Away with a Stranger

Louise Hudson

Dear Charli

Merry Christmas

Louise x

Mounter Press

First Published by Mounter Press 2023

Editing: Aimee Walker Editorial Services

Cover: Coffin Print Designs

eBook ISBN: 978-1-7394180-3-8

Paperback ISBN: 978-1-7394180-2-1

For

LW

Thank you for making me a cat auntie.
Getting to look after the boys when you go on holiday is an absolute pleasure. They're both so special and have left paw prints on my
heart.

&

CW

This book wouldn't be what it is without you.
Your commitment and enthusiasm for this story has been 100% since I shared it with you.
I appreciate every single voice note, every single message.
You rock...

A Note From Louise

Away with a Stranger is a steamy holiday romance containing strong language and sexual scenes. Readers who may be sensitive to this content please take note.

Louise x

Chapter One

Gabriel

A steady stream of colleagues passes my window; it's the same every December, half of us stay and half of us go. I'm always part of the fifty per cent that stay behind, because I've never been to the office Christmas party, not in all the years I've worked here. My obligations are far more important than a free bar and a turkey dinner that tastes like it's been vacuumed packed for deep space exploration. Instead, every year I make the journey back to Christmas Common, the place I grew up, the place I called home for eighteen years of my life but only for birthdays, weddings and Christmases since.

'Back to Bethlehem, is it?' Lawrence raps on the glass pane next to my office door.

'If you mean, am I going home for Christmas, then yes. You ask me this every year.'

Lawrence has worked here for as long as I have, which is eight years too many. Still, accounting is as good a profession as any, and when you work in accounting for the fashion industry, the budget for seasonal parties is high.

'Yeah, but the thing is...' he continues.

I drop my pen to my desk and lean back in my chair to hear what excuse he has for me this time. 'Go on...'

'June's about to drop and I can't be getting hammered. What if she goes into labour? She'd kill me. We've not even been married a year. I can't do it to her. So, my space is going free.'

I purse my lips, jutting out my chin in contemplation. I won't lie, I think about going every single year, but every year, home wins.

'Amelia is going. She couldn't have made it anymore obvious she fancies you if she tried. She didn't buy anyone else a Black Forest hot chocolate last week.'

I knit my brows together. She could have offered to bathe me in it for all I care. I'm not interested. And that's not just in Amelia, it's in anyone.

'Thanks, but I've really got to go home.'

Lawrence forces his hands into his suit pockets and nods. 'Okay, worth a try. You deserve a bit of happiness though, Gabriel. Merry Christmas.'

My chest tightens. Lawrence doesn't know what he's talking about. I glance down at my paperwork and when I look back up, he's gone. I had a bit of happiness once, and then I didn't, and if I truly deserved it, it would have found me again. So, instead, I spend Christmas the only way I know how. The memories may be bittersweet, but unless I cling on to them, I have nothing.

Penny

It's official, no more boring office admin until the new year. For the next couple of weeks I'm nobody's personal assistant. To be even more precise...I'm nobody's anything. The rain flicks up from the pavement as I trudge along the street. I had to park far from the flat again because our spaces were taken. I say our spaces. They haven't been *our* spaces for a while now. Not since Henry left, leaving me, the jilted bride, two months before the fairy-tale Christmas Day wedding I'd always dreamed of. He was my childhood sweetheart and to hear that he just didn't think he could go through with it broke my heart.

My phone pings loudly, and it's a message no one wants: a video of their parents doing the 'Cha Cha Slide' on their Mexican all-inclusive holiday. When they found out the wedding was off, they commiserated by booking a holiday for themselves, but vowed to be back in time for Christmas Day, just in case I needed them. I think deep down they're hoping Henry will come to his senses, but as the date gets ever closer the likelihood of that gets slimmer by the day. The only person who can make me happy this Christmas is me and I'm desperate to find my Christmas joy, because up until now it's been in short supply.

I grind to a halt beside the brick wall of the flat and focus on the cars parked parallel. One belongs to Henry and the other to my best friend, Molly. I can barely drag my eyes away as I hurry along the path. There's odd and there's this. He said he was coming to collect the last of his belongings at some point, but this is completely out of the blue.

I force my key into the lock. That's weird. I rattle it repeatedly, desperately trying to turn it... It's like someone's... I lurch forward as the door flies back on its hinges, and there stands Henry with a suitcase.

'Penny.' He nods.

'My key wouldn't work.' I screw my face up as I glance at it in my palm.

'I know, I've changed the locks.'

'Y-You've done what?' I shriek.

'My parents kicked me out. I have to stay here. You can go to your parents, they'll always have you back.'

I frown in disbelief. Henry's parents are good people, they'd never kick him out. Unless he'd done something awful, but even then, I just can't imagine it.

'They kicked you out? No, they wouldn't do that. Let me talk to them.'

Henry forces the suitcase towards me. 'No, you've done enough, it's because of you that I'm in this mess.'

'Me!' I cry. 'You broke up with me and I still don't know why. We were supposed to be getting married in six days...six days, Henry, and I'm still none the wiser.' I clutch at my forehead, as the droplets of rain hit me. I turn out to the street and the amber glow of the streetlights beam down on my best friend's car.

'Wait. What's Molly's car doing here?'

As I turn back, I spot the shadow in the hall, moving ever closer towards Henry, and as soon as our eyes meet, I know.

'No...' I whisper.

'P-Pen,' Molly stammers as we come face to face at the front door.

'Please don't tell me... No, you wouldn't.'

She swallows hard as she searches frantically for an answer.

I tighten my grip around my keys, the cold, hard metal piercing my skin. Molly shakes her head, and her eyes fill with tears.

'I'm so sorry,' she whispers. 'We didn't mean for you to find out like this.'

My lips part, and a verbal response to the shock is desperate to escape. But nothing. I'm stunned into silence by the betrayal of the two people I'm closest to in the world.

'How long?' I force out.

Henry's jaw locks defiantly.

'How long?' I cry. 'I want the truth.'

My heart crumples as they look to each other for rescue. Because now it's Henry and Molly, not Henry and Penny.

'Longer than we've been apart,' Henry says, reluctantly.

'Henry!' Molly cries, burying her head in her hands. If she's looking for sympathy, she's barking up the wrong tree. The cheating...

'What? She wanted the truth.'

I wrench my suitcase from his hands and that's when my stomach really drops.

Billy...

'Give me my cat!'

'He's our cat!' Henry cries.

'Not anymore!'

I barge forward and storm through the hall. Pausing next to the cupboard under the stairs, I yank open the door and pull out the cat carrier. Me and Billy are out of here. Luckily for me he's the only cat in the world that loves a cat carrier. It clatters to the floor and the ping of a latch echoes through the hall and right on cue, Billy appears.

'Sorry, baby, we've got to go, Daddy's got you a wicked stepmum.'

'Grow up, Pen.' Henry snaps.

'Don't call me that. Never call me that ever again. You lost the right to do that when you slept with someone else.'

I turn, swinging the cat carrier in rage. I open my mouth, but nothing comes out as my throat goes dry. This is the worst Christmas ever.

Henry stumbles back as I march straight for the door, pausing as I catch sight of the large red envelope on the console table by the door. *Our pre-wedding mini break.* His wedding gift...to me. They wouldn't?

I snatch the envelope and tuck it under my arm.

'Hey, what do you think you're doing?'

Grabbing the suitcase with my spare hand, I turn and look between them both. 'Taking what's mine and not someone else's.'

Tears stream down my cheeks as I struggle along the path. I refuse to let them see the pain they have caused me. As I get to the car, I tear open the envelope and key the address into my phone. Three hours!

Fuck it. I don't care. The further I get from Henry and Molly the better. Who cares if I'm on my own, I have Billy and that's all that matters.

Chapter Two

Penny

This is a little further than I'd like to travel, but as I leave the motorway and slip on to the winding country lanes, I realise that this is shaping up to be the Christmas escape I need. The streetlights become that little bit further apart and the night sky a little less polluted. According to the navigation, I'm yards away. I spot the church and a tiny row of cottages, and I think I know exactly my destination. I grind to halt and peer through the windscreen. *Mistletoe Cottage*. Perfect.

Stepping out on to the shingle lane, I cast my eyes above to the sparkling sky. The kind of night sky that's ideal for sharing with another on those long, cold winter evenings. Except the only person I'll be sharing this opulent view with, is Billy. My body's numb – if I hadn't just experienced gut-wrenching betrayal, I'd put it down to the icy December air. I take my small suitcase and holdall from the boot and gently unbuckle the cat carrier from the front seat.

'Come on, Bill, let's get you inside before you remember what it was like to be an outdoor cat.'

I stand at the small swing gate and scan along the roof, taking in the age of the property, along with how overgrown everything is. It's almost like they weren't expecting guests. The pictures online looked a lot more desirable than this. Still, I don't need more than a place to lay my head and a comfy couch to watch Christmas films and eat piles of snacks. It may have been two months since Henry and I broke up, but it's only been three hours since I discovered the depths of his deceit and copious amounts of wine and chocolate are required immediately. I struggle through the gate with Billy in one hand and my luggage in the other, wobbling along the bushy pathway, but as I reach for the bell, I stumble, the cat carrier goes flying and I land in a heap on the cute welcome mat. *Great, they're going to think I'm an idiot.*

Gabriel

Peace and tranquillity. Exactly how I like it.

I drop to the firm, hard seat of the rocking chair and kick back with a very large, very deserving glass of whiskey. I pause and look towards the door and shake my head. It's so noisy at home compared to here, it takes me days to adjust and remind myself that I'm probably hearing things.

I arch my brows as the warm amber liquid passes my lips and hits the back of my throat. *That sure has some bite.* I always like to start the Christmas season this way; it eases me back in, settles me into my routine and takes the edge off the memories.

Inhaling deeply, I shudder as I think about the vicarage mere feet away and how as per usual it is full to the rafters with the whole family. You couldn't even pay me to stay there. I absolutely adore my parents, but as for everyone else, seeing them for Christmas Day lunch is enough. Wrapping paper explosions, gorging on snacks before dinner, watching reruns of classic sitcoms that have no place being televised in today's society. No, that is not a bit of me. I don't even have a tree and that suits me down to the ground – one less thing to worry about when I leave and return to London.

What the hell is that? My eyes flick back towards the door.

I reluctantly drag myself from my reclined position and grab hold of a poker from the fireplace. It's relatively safe around these parts, but you can never be too careful. I take a deep breath and swing the door open.

'Oh my god!' Her high-pitched scream shatters the blissful calm of the cottage and I'd even hazard a guess it woke the whole village.

'Who are you?' I ask before dropping the poker back to my side.

'Penny!' She clambers up slowly from the welcome mat.

She's breathless, looks like she's participated in a twenty-four hour crying contest, and I've absolutely no clue what she's doing here.

'Can I help you?'

'Yes, thank you so much.' She thrusts her holdall towards me, smoothing her long blonde hair back from her face.

'Woah, woah. You've lost me,' I say, holding both hands up in defence.

'Oh sorry.' She rummages deep in her pockets before producing a rather crumpled red envelope. She forces a small yet confident smile and that's when my stomach sinks. *She's meant to be here.*

'Here you go,' she says, thrusting the envelope up to my face.

My eyes widen as I scan the booking confirmation. *No way.*

'I-I think there's been a mistake,' I mutter, rubbing the back of my neck.

Right on cue, my mother and father appear at the gate and grind to a halt, realising they're too late.

'Gabriel!' my mother cries. 'We forgot to—'

'Take the cottage off the lettings site. I know. Miss?'

She looks at me with confusion. 'Hastings. Penny Hastings.'

'Miss Hastings these are my parents Reverend and Mrs Harris.'

My mother shakes her head and tuts. 'Call me Margaret and this is Charles.' She takes Penny and holds her tightly at arm's length. 'I'm so sorry. Our son, Gabriel, has the cottage every Christmas. My husband forgot to de-list it this year.'

'I've got enough to do, Margaret,' my father wails.

My mother throws him 'the look' because being the wife of a reverend comes with a lot of responsibility, but managing pastoral lettings is clearly not his priority, especially at the most important time of the year.

'Y-You mean I can't stay?' Penny whimpers. 'I've travelled nearly three hours.'

'Your insurance will cover it,' I say.

'It was a gift... I don't have insurance.'

Who the hell doesn't have insurance?

'You'll have to go home I'm afraid.' I push my hands into the warm pockets of my grey joggers and stand firm at the threshold.

Tears stream down Penny's cheeks and I hold my breath for what's about to come next.

'I don't have a home to go back to.'

Fuck.

My mother's eyes narrow and I become uncomfortable very quickly, because I know for a fact there is zero room in the vicarage.

'Is it only you, the booking was for two?' my mother asks.

Two? No way am I having a couple under this roof, rubbing my face in their Christmas joy.

'No. It's just me now,' she says, dropping her chin to her chest.

Relief hits me. One is better than two, but none would be preferable.

'Right!' my mother cries. 'Step back, Gabriel, let her in.' She flits her hand towards me and my heart sinks. *How is this even happening?*

Penny wipes her face frenziedly, and her mouth curls into the smallest smile as she looks up at me with apprehension.

'There's only one bed,' my father says in horror.

'Oh, yes. So, there is. There must be a solution...ah...' My mother thinks out loud.

Not the camping bed.

'There's a camping bed, Charles.'

Fan-bloody-tastic. 'Yes, there's the camping bed,' I repeat reluctantly.

'Ah yes, that old thing,' my father says. 'Couldn't have had you two sharing a bed now, could we?'

My grip on her holdall tightens. It's been so long since I've shared a bed with anyone.

Penny dries her eyes, and her breath shakes as she looks to me. 'Stay here together? But we're strangers and this is the middle of nowhere.'

'Oh, don't worry, you'll be completely safe with Gabriel,' my mother tries to reassure her.

'Completely.' *Because we'll be spending no time together.*

'Do I get the bed or the camping bed?' she asks warily.

I burst out laughing. She's disturbed my Christmas, is she for real? 'The camping—'

'Gabriel!' my mother snaps.

'The bed.' I roll my eyes.

We all exchange awkward glances before Penny finally nods.

'Perfect.' My mother clasps her hands together loudly. 'Gabriel, see you tomorrow. Penny, lovely to meet you, we'll leave you in Gabriel's hands.'

She loops her arm through my father's and practically drags him back along the path before he can utter another word.

Penny laughs nervously, and I quickly step back to welcome her in, but she disappears into the darkness of a nearby bush. She fumbles around for what feels like forever and when she reappears, if I wasn't already in mourning for the Christmas I thought I was going to have, this has now made it a million times worse. The booking may have originally been for two, but there was no mention of this.

Chapter Three

Gabriel

My skin prickles as she clings to the tiny prison in her arms, whilst staring at me like I have two heads. There could be anything inside that crate, but I pray it's not what I think it is.

'What is that?'

'It's a cat carrier,' she puffs out.

'G-Get it out,' I stammer.

Her eyes sparkle and her grin widens as she motions to flick the lock open.

'Not the cat. The carrier,' I force out.

Her face falls as she pulls the ball of fur into her arms. 'His name's Billy. Or Sir William to you, until you become acquainted.'

'It could be Sir Elton John for all I care. And we won't be becoming acquainted because he can't be in here. He needs to go.'

Her stance widens and she's bending, completely bending, until the cat is on the floor. 'Oops, he's out now.' She shrugs.

He stalks towards me, circling me, eyeing me up, assessing the status quo. His eyes burn into me and every part of me tenses. I stumble back, blindly searching for protection, for anything that will put some distance between me and this predator. His eyes narrow and that's when I know he doesn't like me. 'He's angry. Why's he angry? He's staring at me.'

She flits around the room, completely unaware of the stand-off taking place only feet away.

'He isn't angry, that's just his face. He's a bit grumpy sometimes, he's an old man now.'

Is that supposed to make me feel sorry for him?

'Penny, I-I'm allergic, you need to keep him away from me.'

I'm not allergic, not even a little bit. I could roll around in animal fur until the cows come home without the need for even a whiff of an antihistamine. The reality is, I'm terrified. Ever since I was viciously attacked by a black cat one Halloween. I still have a small scar on my ankle as a reminder. No, me and cats, we don't mix. And at the age of twenty-eight no one will convince me otherwise.

Her brow wrinkles and she steps towards the kitchen island that separates the room, and is currently the only thing keeping Billy from me. Under the stark lights of the kitchen, she assesses me. 'You're not that allergic though, he hasn't touched you, and you're fine.'

My jaw clenches and my fists ball. She's not going to relent and just roll over. Unlike Billy who's now dragging himself along the kitchen rug.

'My throat feels scratchy,' I croak.

She completely disregards my statement and continues to unpack her life across my lounge. 'He likes male company, you know, he adored Henry.'

'Henry? Who's Henry?'

She pauses, like she's unaware of what she's even said. 'Oh, he was the person I was supposed to be coming here with, but let's just say things didn't work out.' She wheels her suitcase through the middle of the room, stopping right by the kitchen island.

My mouth becomes dry as I attempt to think of a reply, but I have nothing. Whatever her sorry circumstance, she'll just have to toughen up, because sometimes shit hits the fan and you have to deal with it. I know I did. Glancing down at my feline foe, I stretch my leg as far as humanly possible and gently nudge him with my foot until he manoeuvres back into an upright position. As soon as he spots her, he's off, straight to her side.

'Oh, my Billy Bear.' Bending down, she scoops him into her arms and pulls him tightly into her chest. A muffled sound escapes their embrace, and I can't even be sure which of them it came from. Either way one of them is making unnecessary noise, and I can't deal with that for the next...

'How long were you supposed to be staying again?' I ask, trying to figure out how long I'm going to have to avoid this cat.

'Until the twenty-third.'

I tense at the very thought. *Four painfully long nights and three excruciating days.* I wander towards the closet and tug hard on the aged wooden door. Where's the damn camping bed? As soon as I clock it every one of my muscles starts to ache from the sight alone.

'Are you sure you don't want the camping bed? It looks very inviting.'

'No, absolutely not. I want what I've paid for.' She glares.

'Paid for...you said this was a gift! And besides, we don't accept pets, you're in breach of the rental agreement already.'

She halts her unpacking and turns to face me, her stare pinning me to the spot. 'But it's Christmas.'

'I know what time of year it is because I stay here every year...alone.'

Her eyes narrow. 'I can't imagine why.'

My heart begins to race, blood fuelling my system, spurring me on. I could stop this at any moment, but she's pushing every one of my buttons, and I just know she knows it.

'Really? Well, I'm starting to see why this Henry guy bailed.'

She drops her bag back to the couch with a thud and her eyes glisten. A lump forms in my throat and I'm hit with regret as tears fall one by one down her cheeks. The nerve I just hit, runs deep.

'You don't know what you're talking about...'

'I—'

'I want to go to my room. Where is it?'

'First door on the right.' I point towards the ceiling.

She picks up her multiple bags and struggles towards the staircase.

'Here, let me help you,' I offer.

'I've got it,' she mumbles.

Her feet thump on every stair and her anger and upset radiate throughout the cottage. I force my hands into my pockets and lean back against the kitchen island. I didn't think things could get much worse, but clearly, they can. I swallow hard as her words echo back to me. *You don't know what you're talking about.* The problem is, I think I do.

Penny

This is the room from hell.

What was Henry thinking when he booked this? Oh wait, he probably wasn't – too busy thinking about Molly. Moonlight spills through the slit in the curtain and illuminates the huge Victorian wardrobe that resembles the entrance to Narnia. I shudder as to what I might find behind those doors. I'm going to have to look at some point though, because I will be unpacking; I'm not going to let Gabriel ruin this for me. He's not going to dampen the little Christmas spirit I have left. He can say what he likes about the reasons I'm here alone, he has absolutely no idea. Like hell I'll be sharing them with him either, he's already formed a judgement about me, I can tell. Like I have of him. My mind casts to the camping bed and I wonder how his large frame could ever cope on something so small. When I glanced up at him from the welcome mat, I thought I'd come face to face with a giant. Never before have I seen a man so tall and broad, with caramel-blond hair, he's like a real-life Greek god. Unfortunately, he's also rude and aloof, which completely trumps his brooding good looks. Never before have I met someone with so little Christmas cheer, I mean there's not even a tree up. I roll to my side and stretch out in search of Billy, but the place he occupied when we first went to bed is now cold. I bolt upright, holding the sheets tightly around me, shielding my body from the chill. A slither of light shines through the crack in the door and my stomach churns. Oh no...my boy is inquisitive and there's nothing he loves more than new people. And if I know Billy, there's only one place he'll be.

Chapter Four

Gabriel

The camping bed creaks, and it is the worst. I don't know what my mother was thinking. Oh wait, yes I do. Single son. Single female. Simple math. There's nothing simple about it though, not where I'm concerned. I don't think there's been one Christmas in the last eight years when she hasn't tried to set me up with someone. The harder she tries the more I push against it. Luckily, I always have the same excuse why getting involved with anyone would not be practical: the church nativity. My parents will never question my commitment to that. What I need is no drama, no disturbances, no distractions, and I've been successful in my quest, until now. The look on Penny's face as she dragged herself upstairs earlier has plagued my thoughts ever since. There's more to her story than she's letting on and somewhere deep inside a part of me wants to know, but the moment I let her in to more than my home is when the problems will start. I have to keep her and that cat at arm's length and as long as I keep reminding myself why I come home every year, everything will be fine.

I close my eyes, inhaling deeply, a tried and tested method for falling asleep when you're agitated, yet for some reason tonight it's failing me. My eyes ping open as a soft thud emanates from the stairs and I shoot glances in every direction, it sounded chillingly familiar, yet I can't see a...

'Oh no. No. No. No. Get off me,' I grind out, my back pinned to the coarse fabric of the bed. 'No, don't you dare...sit.' The tremor of my breath is heavy as Billy's tail swishes back and forth, his beady little eyes glaring down at me. This is a living hell and the devil himself has just taken up residence on my chest. My breathing is so rapid that on every in-breath the damn thing rises by about an inch and it's not even budging. The tell-tale knock of the bannisters signals that help is on the way, but it's nowhere near quick enough.

'P-Penny. P-Penny.' My voice cracks as my throat goes dry. From my supine position, I can scarcely make out her outline as she looms over me, tiptoeing like a burglar.

'Billy...Billy, get off him,' she hisses. 'Gabriel, I'm so sorry. Here, I'll take him. I can't really see though. It's a bit dark.'

'Fine, just hurry and be careful of the bed, don't lean—'

The frame crunches and as the first leg buckles, so follows the second, swiftly followed by the third and fourth, before the whole thing comes crashing down. A chilling squeal escapes her lips and Billy scarpers, leaving a trail of destruction in his wake. Splintered wood surrounds me as I lie, bruised and in pain, in the remains of what was supposed to be my bed for the next few nights.

'Oh my god. I'm so sorry. Oh god. I can't say god, can I? Not here. Oh Christ. Oh, I can't mention him either. I didn't know the door was open and he got out.'

'Really?' I say, tipping my chin towards her.

She wraps her arms around her body and it's only then that I realise how little she wears to bed. I shake my head to eradicate the unwelcome thoughts. I really didn't think things could get any worse. I'd pinch myself in hope that this was all a nightmare. I could believe it if it wasn't for the shooting pain coursing through my body.

'So...where will you sleep now?' she whispers.

Simultaneously, we glance at the tiny two-seater couch that couldn't sleep a child let alone a six-foot man. She scratches her head, then palms at her chest and despite the little light we find ourselves in, I can barely make out the blush streaking across her flesh, but it's definitely there. Only one thought could provoke such a reaction. *This is a terrible idea.*

Penny

'You're touching me.' I huff loudly.

'We're top and tailing, sharing a bed, what do you expect?' Gabriel grinds out.

I need peace and quiet when I sleep, not exasperated heavy breathing. I know if I'd kept a closer eye on Billy that this would never have happened, but there's absolutely no way I'm admitting fault. Not in a million Christmases. Gabriel's calf brushes against me as he turns, and I can't ignore the thickness of his muscles. I've had some misfortune this year, but to find myself in bed with a handsome stranger who's clearly as agitated by my presence as I am his, well, it's the icing on the cake. If luck was finally turning in my favour, he would have swept me off the doorstep in a grand romantic gesture, when instead, it was more of a case of no room at the inn.

'Your brain is too loud,' he mumbles.

'What?'

'I can hear you think, Penny, it's tick, tick, ticking, like a flaming clock.'

'Don't be ridiculous, that's impossible,' I mutter, rolling as far away as humanly possible. I steady myself on the edge of the bed and glance at the time on the quaint carriage clock on the nightstand. I wonder what time he gets up. Will he wake me? Will he bring me breakfast in bed? I scoff out loud as I imagine it.

'What now?' he forces out.

'N-nothing. Sorry.'

Seconds pass into minutes and as I finally think he's fallen asleep, he tuts loudly.

'What now?' I mimic.

'I need the bathroom.'

'TMI, Gabriel. Go then, I'm not stopping you.'

'No, but Gandalf will. He's outside the door, I know it.'

I roll my lips to stifle my smile as I imagine Billy in a cloak and staff, beyond the confines of the bedroom.

'Did he touch you before? Like skin to skin? Your allergies, they're okay?'

'Fine, I just need him to keep his distance.'

I roll my eyes at the dramatics; I've never known anything like it. Allergies, yeah right. My hand grazes his quad as I stretch out, and I retract immediately as he flinches.

'Sorry,' I mutter.

Silence. Deadly silence. I knew sharing the cottage might be awkward, but he's just downright rude. It's no surprise he likes to spend Christmas alone, because with his award-winning personality I can't imagine people are queuing around the block to spend time with him.

'I thought you were going to the bathroom?' I say eventually.

'I'll hold it. It's good for the pelvic floor.'

Oh my god. He didn't just say that. Now I'm imagining all sorts. The way those grey joggers clung to his hips earlier, I bet he's toned to perfection.

'You hold it then. At least we've only got a few nights of this. It could be worse,' I say cheerily.

More silence.

I shake my head. *Like this could get any worse.* I won't let him break me though. I came here to salvage something from my disastrous relationship. I want the Christmas cottage experience I paid for...that Henry paid for. A crippling tightness claws at my chest as I picture their faces, and I wonder how I never saw it before. I deserve a bit of happiness and I'll be damned if I'm going to let Scrooge ruin it for me. I'll leave here full of Christmas joy if it's the last thing I do.

Chapter Five

Gabriel

My back's killing me. And to think I thought the camping bed was bad. It's not surprising since I spent half the night with my head hanging off the end of the mattress staring into the abyss. The cat was right outside the door this morning and shot past me like a bullet as soon as I'd vacated the room. I know the bond between people and their pets is strong, but I swear he's obsessed with her, like literally obsessed. He wasn't interested in me one iota last night. It was a warning, a stark and deadly warning to keep the hell away from his woman. Still, since I ended up in bed with her and he ended up on the other side of the door, I'd say it's one-nil to me.

Sweat trails down my body as I slow towards the cottage door, pushing down forcefully on the handle. The downstairs is exactly how I prefer it.

Empty.

I don't know how we're going to navigate the next few days and nights because sharing a bed is quite frankly absurd.

Absolutely no good can come of it. If I could put a barrier

up straight down the middle, I would. The inadvertent touches were innocent enough, but they riled me. It's not that I don't want her here, it's that I don't want anybody here. And she's quite possibly the worst thing that could have happened, because as I left her sleeping this morning, for the first time I saw how breathtakingly beautiful she is, but in the most infuriating way imaginable. Every time our bodies touched last night, guilt consumed me, because god, what wouldn't I give to throw caution to the wind and say to hell with the consequences, but I can't go there at Christmas ever again. I lean against the kitchen island and stretch out my muscles, because running in winter is bad enough, but when you don't cool down properly, you're asking for trouble, and I can't afford to seize up now.

'Good morning!'

'Jesus...' I stumble back and steady myself against the couch as Penny appears from behind the island armed with a frying pan.

'Why are you hiding behind there?' I cry.

'Oh, I was deep in the cupboard.'

'Can I ask the fuck why?' I say, pulling my t-shirt over my head and rubbing it across my chest.

She stares blankly at me and the frying pan flops to her side.

'B-Billy.' She bends and reappears, holding my feline arch-nemesis. 'He was in the cupboard.'

'Oh, for god's sake get the cat out of the kitchen, Penny.'

She scowls, releasing him to the floor. 'It's not his fault. The kitchen and lounge are in the same room, he doesn't know where his boundaries are.'

I raise my brows in agreement. 'Too bloody right he doesn't.'

She palms mindlessly at her chest and her robe falls open ever so slightly, and I catch the rosiness as it spreads across her body.

'Are you okay?' I step back towards the kitchen island and

toss my t-shirt to the side. Her eyes follow the shirt, then flick back to me.

'A-Are you leaving that there?'

'No. I'm going to put it in the wash, not that it should matter to you.'

'I don't want to live in mess.'

Bloody cheek. 'I'm not messy. It's just a bit more cluttered around here than I'd usually like.'

'Meaning me and Billy?' She strides around the island still clutching the frying pan and I hastily step back.

'If the cat fits.'

'Cap. You mean if the cap fits.' She laughs mockingly.

'Do I?'

We hold each other's stare and relief hits me. The frostiness from last night is well and truly alive and kicking, which is the best possible outcome for our current situation, because anything other than two strangers sharing a cottage, needs to remain off the table.

Her throat bobs as she swallows hard. Choked on her own words, she turns and makes her way back to the stove.

'Well, if that will be all, I'm going to have a shower and then I'm off out, so try and keep yourself out of trouble.'

She drags her eyes towards mine and quickly looks away, not uttering a single word. I smile to myself until I'm out of view and as I reach the top of the staircase, I release the breath I've been holding and gasp for air. My heart pounds in my chest and I slam the bathroom door with force before resting my head against the wood. The sooner this arrangement is over the better, for everyone.

❄

Perched on the stage edge, my feet swing heavily against the wood. The dull thump of my shoes rumbles throughout the hall. I'm waiting for my parents, to hear what delights we have in store for the parish this year. But first I want to know what the hell they were doing, forgetting to book out the cottage, and secondly, why my mother thought it was a good idea to leave a stranger in my company. She knows I hate this time of year more than most and giving me a house guest is possibly the worst idea she's had since she decided to decorate the hall using fake Christmas trees over real ones.

'Gabriel,' my father calls across the hall. My mother trails closely behind and the smile on her face could not be rivalled. She's knows exactly what she's done and is revelling in every last minute.

'How's Penny?' they chime simultaneously.

'Fine,' I force out.

'It must be lovely to have some company for a change,' my mother says.

I shake my head in disbelief. 'Not really. If it wasn't for the nativity, you know I'd stay in London.'

'Gabriel! That's a terrible thing to say. Apologise to your mother.' My father buries his head back in his phone and guilt hits me.

'Sorry, but you know I really prefer my own company. I'd stay with you though, if it wasn't for the twins.'

My divorced brother, Adam, gets his daughters every other Christmas, and it's one of the only times my parents get to see their grandchildren, so they stay in the vicarage, like one big unconventional happy family. The twins give me the creeps, like they could give the girls from *The Shining* a run for their money sort of creepy.

'They're lovely children. I don't know what you're talking about.' My mother slaps me on the arm.

'No...Oh no.' My father clutches at his chest and steps back. We turn towards him, and my mother reaches out to steady him.

'Charles? What's the matter? What is it?'

His face is ashen, and if it wasn't for the fact that my father is fitter than I am, I'd be seriously worried. No, whatever this is, is big, but not life threatening big.

'Lottie Palmer. This year's Mary...she's broken her ankle.' He tugs uncomfortably at his collar.

My heart leaps. It's been a different virgin for the last eight years. When I heard this year it was Lottie Palmer, I could have cried. She's loud, brash and controlling and not Mary material one bit, but my father was prepared to give her a go.

'Oh no, that's terrible. What happened?' I fake concern.

'Massive pothole.'

'Brilliant.' I snigger and my mother throws me a death stare.

'That's one of my parishioners, Gabriel, mind your tone.'

'Oh, come on, Dad, what were you even thinking in the first place?'

His eyes narrow and he steps towards me. I may be taller than him, but he has a presence that makes him seem ten feet tall. 'I was thinking that I've been the reverend of this parish for thirty years and without fail every Christmas I've put on a nativity so popular that people travel for miles. A nativity that I've trusted you to participate in since the year you were born. You may be my son, but you're not bigger than the story we tell – you should be humbled that I still let you hold the role you do.' He backs away and storms towards his office.

A lump rises to my throat. That was brutal. My mother clutches at my arms and I inhale deeply.

'He gets stressed easily, don't take it to heart. Why don't you get back to Penny?'

I smile weakly. That's the last thing I want to do.

Chapter Six

Penny

Try not to get in any trouble.

Famous last words. Except, it's not me who's in trouble. When we're apportioning blame, there's only one person culpable in my eyes and in the distance, I can see him trudging along the lane with what appears to be the weight of the world on his shoulders. Well, things are about to get a hell of a lot worse before they get better. I hold my hand to my forehead, shielding my eyes from the little sunlight, to get a better view of the roof from my current standpoint, but it's no good. I know he's up there, he just won't come down.

'What are you doing?' Gabriel asks as approaches.

'You.' I point. 'You left the bathroom window open.'

'And?' He steps back affronted.

'And...Billy got out. He's an indoor cat, he's up there terrified.'

A grin spreads from ear to ear and Gabriel folds his arms as he joins me in gazing upwards. 'Well, well, how the tables have turned.'

'Get a ladder, you need to get him down,' I cry.

His face falls and he hurries towards the door. 'No way. He'll come down in his own time. He has nine lives, let him live a little. Plus...my allergies.'

'You'll be praying you die of anaphylactic shock if you don't help me get him down.'

He stops as he presses down on the handle and throws an exasperated look across his shoulder. 'Fine.'

I place my hands on my hips and peer upwards just as Billy pokes his head over the gutter.

'Billy! Look, there he is.' I flick my wrist towards the heavens.

Gabriel stands with his phone pressed tightly between his ear and shoulder as he surveys the cottage.

'What are you waiting for?' I hiss.

'Shhhh. I'm getting a ladder.' He presses a finger to his lips and listens intently. 'Hi, Dad, I need a ladder... Don't ask. Look, can you bring one over or not?' He rubs his jaw repeatedly. 'Thanks. See you soon.'

'How long?' I bounce on the spot.

'Five minutes.'

As we stand in silence, I dust the leaves from the path with my foot. If he's going up a ladder the least I can do is make sure the path is clear.

'Leave that, it's pointless,' Gabriel murmurs.

'Leave that, it's pointless,' I mimic under my breath.

'So mature, Penny.'

'So miserable, Gabriel.'

He stiffens, adjusting his shirt as if it's too tight, before rolling his sleeves up to the elbow. Thick veins cord around his forearms, and I've never in my twenty-six years on this planet seen anything like it. I focus on his fingertips as they flex on his hips and for the briefest of seconds, I wonder what they would feel like flexed against me. *Stop it.*

'Where's this flaming ladder,' he mutters, chin raised towards the roof.

Right on cue, Gabriel's parents arrive in single file carrying the ladder between them with a man who looks like Gabriel's double and two adorable girls.

'Why has this turned into a family affair?' Gabriel moans.

'Gabriel, shush. Your father can't carry it on his own and I wanted to introduce Adam and the girls to Penny,' she says, pulling me into a comforting hug.

The ladder clatters against the guttering and Gabriel begins his ascent one rung at a time.

'Hurry,' I plead.

Gabriel throws me a death stare and I practically wither under his gaze. He's intimidating and detached and there should be nothing attractive about it, but he's about to rescue Billy, and despite everything, that might make him a real-life hero.

Gabriel

I swear a lifetime has passed, but in reality, I've been up here minutes.

'Be careful!' my mother cries.

I inhale deeply and close my eyes. Not only do I have to rescue this deadly predator, but I have to do it with a bloody audience.

'Here, give him these!' Penny cries, rattling the ladder.

I cling to the roof tiles, steadying myself. 'What the hell are you doing, you could have had me off, and what the hell are these?'

As I take the packet from her, the offensive odour hits me.

'Fishy Friends?' I bring them a bit closer to my nose. 'Dear god, these are awful.'

'Gabriel!' my father cries.

'Sorry!'

'He loves them,' Penny says, bouncing on the spot.

'I'd bet good money on it he doesn't,' I mutter under my breath.

I wave the packet towards him, and he stares blankly, not even acknowledging my rescue efforts. 'Come on, Billy, come here and have some Fishy Friends and I'll get you back on solid ground.'

'How's it going?' Penny calls.

'Give me a minute.'

I pull my gloves from my pockets and carefully inch them on to my hands. They offer minimal protection, but anything to keep me from being clawed to death. Inaudible chatter breaks out below. When I throw a quick glance across my shoulder, a chill runs through my body as I lock eyes with the twins, who have their gaze trained solely on me.

'Can we pet the cat, Uncle Gabriel?' they call up. Ignoring them, I turn my attention back to Billy. This is exactly the kind of drama I hate.

'Billy, come on, please.' He places one paw tentatively in front of the other and I reach out as far as physically possible without risk of plunging to the cold, hard ground below. My heart rate doubles as my gloved hand connects with his sodden fur, causing my whole body to tense. I can't believe I'm even doing this right now. I pull him into my chest, and he clambers up to my shoulder, digging his claws in for dear life. If he goes for my neck, I swear they'll both be out of here quicker than they arrived. His claws sink deeper, causing a bead of sweat to trickle down my brow, and the squeal of delight from the twins makes my blood run cold.

'Some help here please.' I groan, navigating the ladder in reverse. 'Hello?'

'Oh, Gabriel, how can I ever repay you?' Penny cries and rushes to meet me at the bottom, throwing her arms around a damp, cold Billy.

Leave me in peace. Keep the cat away from me.

'And look, no allergies,' she says, beaming up at me.

'Allergies?' My mother laughs.

I throw her a deadly glare and take her by the elbow, ushering her away. 'Thanks for helping out, you best get back to the hall now along with The Grady twins.'

Adam's eyes narrow and he shakes his head. 'You're a horrible human being, do you know that?'

Penny pauses at the doorway and turns, still cradling Billy in her arms. 'Oh, I'll definitely stop by, Margaret. I'll be more than happy to help and lovely to meet you all.' She waves before heading inside.

I swallow hard. *Help?* No. I can't have her involved. She'd be more of a hindrance.

'Serves you right...' Adam says, rounding up the girls. My mother waves and gives me a subtle wink before making her way back along the path. I turn back to find my father now navigating the ladder alone.

'What did you say to her?' I croak.

'Nothing.'

'Dad? What does she mean by help?'

He shrugs. 'Just chipping in, helping your mother and Adam with decorations, that sort of thing.'

I sag with relief. For a moment I was imagining the worst.

'She could be more help though, Gabriel...'

My throat tightens. 'No...'

'We're running out of time. She's the best candidate.'

'You don't know what you're asking of her...and of me for that matter. Don't my feelings come into this at all?'

He stands before me, eye to eye, man to man, and I know there was never going to be any conversation about this, it's an order, of the highest calling.

'Announce unto her...that she has been chosen.'

'But, Dad...' I swallow hard.

He places the ladder gently on the ground and holds me firmly by the biceps. 'Gabriel, the nativity needs her. I have faith in you. You mark my words, she'll be the best Virgin Mary you've ever had.'

Chapter Seven

Penny

I've been waiting hours to thank Gabriel.

He went straight out for a run after rescuing Billy and as soon as he returned, he locked himself in the bathroom. I've never known a man to soak for as long as he's been in the tub; he'll be like a prune by the time he's out. My mind wanders to dangerous territory as I envisage him emerging like James Bond from the water, droplets trickling down his toned body. I shake my head to pull myself from my trance and sink into the comfort of the bed with Billy nestled in cosily next to me. He's almost recovered from his rooftop exploration, and I dread to think what would have happened if Gabriel hadn't stepped up. The bathroom lock clicks and I push myself up with haste – this is my moment. I take a deep breath and steady my gaze on the doorway and wait.

Nothing.

My jaw drops at the clink of glass in the kitchen. Unbelievable. He went downstairs, without so much as a hello. He's avoiding me and it's not even my fault. He left the window open and only has himself to blame. My pulse quickens as my anger escalates; he needs to take some responsibility. I tear the covers back and Billy scarpers from the bed.

I rip the dressing gown from the back of the door and descend the stairs before I've even finished tying it. As my feet connect with the tiled floor of the downstairs, I notice how warm it now is. The fire pops and I flinch as my eyes dart around the room. It's the most Christmassy the place has been since I arrived, if it wasn't for the lack of tree or decorations it'd be perfect.

'Did you want something?' Gabriel mutters.

He slowly brings a glass of amber liquid to his mouth, as he casually leans back in the rocking chair.

'Y-y-yes.' I clear my throat. 'An apology.'

His laughter is cold and detached and only serves to infuriate me more.

'I don't know what's so funny. Everything that happened today was your fault.'

'My fault?' He leans forward, his stance widening as he rests his elbows on his knees. 'So, it's my fault that you turned up here and disrupted my Christmas with your feral cat and somehow I'm to blame for him ending up on my roof because I left my window open.'

'Exactly.' I fold my arms.

He shakes his head as he downs the remainder of his drink.

'You really don't want us here, do you?' I ask.

'How have you only just worked that out?' He drags himself to his feet and saunters past me, not even daring to look in my direction.

I knew he had the ability to be an arsehole, but he's really stepped it up a gear. My Christmas spirit is waning because he's trampling all over it. Gabriel cares about only himself.

'Fine,' I force out. 'I'll go right now.'

Water splashes as he drops his glass into the washing up bowl and I study the rise and fall of his back. *Say something, anything, damn it.*

'I'd get out while you still can if I were you.'

Arghhh.

My feet pound hard against every stair as I hurry back to the bedroom, discarding the dressing gown wildly across the room. I scoop up every item of clothing I can lay my hands on and force them into my suitcase. There's no point waiting until morning. I arrived here in darkness; I'll leave in darkness.

With Billy under one arm and my suitcase in the other, I hurtle through the cottage without pausing for breath. This vacation is over.

'Where are you going?' he sighs as I drag my case behind me.

'Getting out whilst I still can. Apparently.'

'Penny, wait.'

I throw the cottage door back on its hinges and struggle along the path.

'Penny—'

'It doesn't surprise me that you stay here every year on your own, because no one in their right mind would want to spend Christmas with you.'

His jaw locks tight, as he inhales sharply. I stare at him, expecting a scathing comeback, but instead he leans forward and opens my car door. *Unbelievable.*

I place the cat carrier on the passenger seat and by the time I've secured it in place, the boot slams hard.

'I put your case in the boot. Drive safely and have a good Christmas, Penny.'

I shake my head, confused by his words. We've just come to loggerheads over this absolute fucked-up situation and he's told me to drive safely and have a good one. Henry didn't even do that, and we shared a whole lot more than a cottage and a bed for one night.

'Thanks,' I force out, dragging my eyes away and sliding into the driver's seat.

He pushes the door closed behind me and stands with his hands in his pockets, waiting. For what, I don't know. He probably wants to make sure I actually leave.

I press down on the clutch and hit the start button, but the engine chokes and cuts out. *Fuck.* I hit the start button again and the same. My stomach sinks as I try to recall the last time I put petrol in, but one thing I do know is that I didn't put any in during my three-hour car journey here. *Double fuck.*

I open the car door and drag the cat carrier behind me.

'Do you want me to get your case?' Gabriel asks.

I throw him a sideways glance and march back along the path. Tonight is going to be torture.

Gabriel

No one in their right mind would want to spend Christmas with you.

Her words cut deep. Too deep for a stranger.

I stare into the emptiness beside me. At some point between closing my eyes and opening them, she disappeared, and I find myself waking up alone. It's not the first time this has happened, but this stings particularly hard, because I'm not supposed to care. In a desperate attempt to save myself from a repeat of history, I pushed her away with my heartless words. I never expected my gut to twist as she flew out the door last night; that's when I realised that perhaps I'd made a huge mistake and the fact my stomach resettled as soon as the engine failed to start only confirmed it. I didn't care that she wouldn't look me in the eye as she slipped into bed beside me, or that she promptly turned away so we didn't have to speak. All that mattered was that she was still here.

Now all I need is to summon the courage to ask her to be more than the stranger sleeping in my bed, I need her to be Mary. For the first time in my twenty-eight years I saw fear in my father's eyes that the nativity might not go ahead. If I wasn't so stubborn, I'd have had this wrapped up last night, but here I am, alone and Mary-less.

I drag myself from the bed, my legs heavy as they trudge down the stairs. I shield my eyes as stark daylight beams through the kitchen window, yesterday things were positively dreary, but this is unusually bright. I scan the room for any sign of her, my eyes dropping to the mat by the front door, and I'm hit by the noticeable absence of her boots. *Shit.* I stride towards the door and yank it open.

'Gabriel!' She stumbles back.

I reach out to her, but it's too late and she topples backwards with a familiar crunch.

It's then that the brightness registers, as she lands in a cushion of the deepest snow I've seen in years.

The iciness bites at my bare chest, and I stoop forward and rescue her as she attempts to pull herself free.

'Are you okay?'

'Why aren't you dressed?' she snaps.

'Were you trying to leave again?'

She dusts the snow from her winter coat and pushes brashly past me. 'What with no petrol and snow deeper than the Siberian desert? No, I was off to the church hall. I might as well honour my offer to help, since I'm stuck here.'

Despite the fact she's as frosty as the weather, relief hits me that she's staying.

'I'll get dressed then and clear the path. We can go to the hall together?' I suggest.

She slams the kettle back on to its base, aggressively hitting the switch. 'I don't need a chaperone. And you clearly want to be on your own, so don't put yourself out.'

Fuck, she's angry. She's never going to agree to be Mary at this rate. 'I need to go myself anyway, so we might as well go together.'

'Fine. Whatever.' She waves her hand dismissively, turning her back to me.

I take the stairs slowly as I struggle to control the race of my pulse. God, she gets me going and in a way I never imagined a mere stranger could. I breathe a sigh of relief as my back hits the closed bedroom door, putting some firm distance between us. What this means, hell, I wish I knew, but there's only one thing I'm certain of – I don't want to be the man that no one wants to spend Christmas with, especially Penny.

Chapter Eight

Penny

The hall is eerily quiet. Margaret told me this was the biggest and best nativity for absolute miles, but it looks more like a shut down film set. Props in disarray, Christmas trees half erected, garlands hanging haphazardly from the ceiling. Something is off and I don't need to have been here before to work that out.

Gabriel has been tight-lipped from the moment we arrived. Why he's even here I don't know, he's been completely cryptic about this whole production. If it wasn't for Margaret and Reverend Harris, I wouldn't have a clue. 'What's going on here?' I ask him across my shoulder.

'Just some minor setbacks.'

Minor.

'Ah you've made it! Wonderful, wonderful!' Reverend Harris calls as he strides across the hall. He pulls me into a tight embrace and Gabriel's eyes widen in horror.

'Lovely to see you, Reverend.'

'Oh, call me Charles, please. You'll never know how grateful we are, everyone is so pleased to have you—'

'Dad, a word,' Gabriel forces out, prising me from his father's arms.

Charles pales and pulls at his collar. 'Oh...Gabri—'

I stand transfixed as Gabriel pulls his father away, and the inaudible exchange between them makes my stomach flip. They're talking about me. Uneasiness weighs heavy as I start to explore the hall. He still wants me to leave, I know it; he may not have said anything about it since last night, but now I'm snowed in, he's desperate. He's asking him for a Christmas miracle, to rid me from the cottage for good. It's the only logical explanation to his presence here this morning.

'Hello!' I turn and my eyes drop to the twins I met yesterday. Sisters speaking in perfect unison should be endearing, but it might be the creepiest thing I've ever witnessed.

'Hi...girls.'

They beam up at me, their linked arms swinging back and forth at an alarming trajectory.

'Are you looking forward to Christmas?' I ask.

They turn to one another and their faces fall. *Oh hell, what have I said?*

They shake their heads, their solemn expressions worsening. I crouch down to my knees until we're eye level and take one of each of their hands. 'Why not? There's so much to look forward to. I've had a terrible year and even I'm looking forward to it.' My heart lifts slightly at my own words, because anything is better than being with a man who lies and cheats and breaks your heart, even staying with a miserable Scrooge.

Margaret told me their names yesterday, but I'll be damned if I know who's who. Leaning back to take them both in, I hold my breath as I hope I get this right. 'Holly?'

'Yes?' The twin on the right says. *Phew*. 'Why aren't you looking forward to Christmas?'

'If the nativity doesn't go ahead then we don't get to see Monty the donkey.'

I frown, turning towards the other twin, who by process of elimination must be Izzy. 'Why wouldn't the nativity go ahead?'

They exchange nervous glances, clearly about to spill why everything is completely up in the air.

'Girls?'

'Daddy said it's a secret, but we overheard Nanny Margaret talking to Grandad Charles this morning,' Holly whispers.

I lean in closer. 'Go on, you can tell me.'

'Lottie Palmer broke her ankle and now can't be in the nativity and Grandad told Uncle Gabriel that he had to make an announcement and this morning Nanny said that he shouldn't have asked him and now Grandad and Uncle Gabriel are arguing about it.'

My mind races at a million miles an hour, processing the tea that's just spilt from Holly's tiny mouth, and I blink rapidly in an attempt to decipher her interpretation of the facts.

'So someone needs to replace Lottie, and Gabriel's supposed to tell everyone who the replacement is?'

Izzy elbows Holly hard and shakes her head.

'Yes, but he won't ask her because he doesn't want her to do it.'

I may not have been here very long, but I've seen zero other women that may be able to take on a role in this nativity and there's only one person I can think of that Gabriel would refuse to ask. My mouth goes dry as I look desperately for an adult to clear up the confusion.

'Girls...is it me?'

They both nod and a mixture of sadness and anger bursts inside of me. I can't believe that Gabriel would jeopardise the whole nativity because he wants me gone. Well, I've got exactly nowhere else to be, and if I can put a smile on these girls faces and keep the biggest and best nativity in production, then to hell with his feelings, I'm going to do it.

'Don't worry, girls, you'll get to see Monty.'

I scramble to my feet and speed through the hall. 'Charles... Gabriel...' I shout, my voice echoing through the empty corridor. A door flies open, springing back on the hinges, and Gabriel emerges, his face dropping as soon as he sees me.

'What's the matter?'

'You...' I point. 'You weren't even going to ask me, were you?'

His eyes widen and he opens his mouth to speak before closing it abruptly.

'Cat got your tongue?'

His jaw locks tightly, and he shakes his head. 'How did you? It's not like that.'

'Oh really. Well, I don't need you to ask me. I'll do it, whatever Lottie Palmer was doing, I'll be her replacement.' I peer across his shoulder and Charles beams back at me.

'God bless you, Penny.'

Gabriel shakes his head and swallows hard. 'Are you sure? It's not for everyone, Penny. Think about this before you say yes.'

'You're trying to talk me out of it because you don't want me to do it.'

His steely eyes hold mine and for a second, I think they soften, and my stomach somersaults.

'It's not that at all. I don't want you to commit to something you can't see through.'

If only he knew how committed I really can be. In four days I was supposed to be vowing my life to someone else, now I'm pledging to a nativity instead. 'If I say I'm going to do something, I'm going to do it.'

Gabriel drops his eyes to the floor and nods. 'Okay. Thank you.'

'I'm not doing this for you, I'm doing it for the twins and some donkey called Monty.'

'Wonderful.' Charles clasps his hands together and links his arm in mine. 'I'll get Helen to provide you a costume, she might need to adjust it for your measurements.'

Excitement courses through my veins. 'I've not performed in anything since school, I'd never have imagined having a little part in a village nativity.'

Charles laughs softly and pats my arm. 'I'd hardly call the Virgin Mary a little part now.'

I clear my throat and grasp mindlessly at the collar of my t-shirt. 'The Virgin—'

'Mary,' Gabriel repeats. 'Are you sure you're okay with this? It's not too late.'

'No. I'm fine...I just...I'm fine.' There's no way I'm backing out now. I can do this. And if it keeps me occupied and out of Gabriel's hair it's a bonus all round.

'Great. We have a rehearsal tomorrow. Here's your lines, try and get some practice in and then we can take it from there. Gabriel will help.' My jaw drops open as Charles thrusts the script into my hand.

'Shouldn't I rehearse with someone else, like, I don't know, Joseph?' I call after Charles, but he's already disappeared along the corridor.

I turn to Gabriel, and he rolls his lips as he tries to contain his smile.

'What? What aren't you telling me?'

He steps forward. 'You want to rehearse with Joseph?'

'It makes sense, don't you think? What good are you to me?' I snap.

He laughs, and it's low and seductive and touches parts of me I'm not expecting. Nervous anticipation grips me as I bring myself to ask the question.

'Who's Joseph?'

Lowering his head, he drops his mouth next to my ear and whispers, 'I am.'

Chapter Nine

Gabriel

I don't think I've ever experienced hostility like it.

We've sat in silence since we returned to the cottage and despite having her head buried in a book and Billy sat snuggly on her lap, I know her mind is firmly on the nativity.

When I confessed my true role to her in a lowly whisper, I was close enough to see the hairs prickle on her arms and the skin on her neck ripple into goosebumps. She's as apprehensive about this as I am. Sharing a stage and a bed might be too close for comfort for both of us. I admire her tenacity though, she was prepared to go through with this, with or without me asking, and that takes some courage.

I haven't had a Mary that I knew beyond the sharing of a script in over eight years. In fact, I never thought I'd share a bed with a Mary ever again, but fate had other ideas.

I glance to where she rocks casually in the corner. Usually I'd be annoyed that she's taken my chair, but I like seeing her in it. As my eyes burn into her, she drags her face to meet mine.

'What? Am I rocking too loudly? Breathing irregularly?'

I shake my head and look away.

'Come on you must have something to say, you usually do,' she says, goading me.

'There's no point talking if you're going to be like this. We can talk when you've calmed down.' I stand, removing myself from the situation.

'Calmed down?' She launches forward from the chair and Billy flies from her lap. 'Calmed down?'

'I heard you the first time,' I grind out as I ascend the stairs two at a time to escape her wrath.

'When I realised you hadn't asked me to be in the nativity, I thought it was because you didn't want me staying any longer than necessary in the cottage, but to find out it's because you didn't want to star opposite me, that's plain rude. You barely know me! What were you hoping for, a better, more qualified Mary to ride into town, someone who ticks all of your boxes?'

She's officially gone nuclear. There's no stopping her now as she backs me uncomfortably into the bedroom.

'I don't know where you're getting this all from. I never once said any of these things.'

'You didn't have to, it's been written all over your face since the moment I arrived and now you know you're stuck with me, you gave me the big seductive *I am* in the hall earlier. So, let's get one thing straight, you might be blessed with the looks of an angel, Gabriel Harris, but your personality rivals the devil, and if you think for one second that anything more than sleeping is going to be happening in this bed you've got another think coming. I am nobody's understudy, I'm the damn lead.'

My back hits the wall as she crowds me, and fuck, I don't think I've ever been more turned on and terrified at the same time.

'I hear you,' I force out.

She charges towards the bedroom door and pauses to look back at me. 'And Billy's sleeping in here. Allergies my arse.'

I bite my tongue to stop myself from saying anything further. Releasing a huge breath, I drop to the foot of the bed and throw myself back against the covers. I'm a royal idiot. I spent too long procrastinating over the whole thing and now I've made it a million times worse. If I want to salvage more than a trip to Bethlehem over the next few days, I'm going to have try and put the past behind me. A high-pitched meow sounds from the bedroom door and I drag my eyes towards Billy, who's clearly on top of the world about the impending sleeping arrangements. There's only one way back into Penny's good books and I'm staring right at him.

Penny

My nose twitches as a heavenly scent passes through the cottage. I must be dreaming because I haven't smelt anything this divine since I arrived. Pressing my fingertips into my eye sockets, I rub repeatedly until I can open them enough to allow the daylight in. I'm greeted by Billy's beautiful face and he headbutts me lovingly. I've missed these morning wake-up calls the last few days. When I eventually came to bed last night Gabriel was fully clothed and fast asleep on the edge of the bed, and if I'm honest it was a welcome relief.

Because staying angry with such a handsome specimen of a man takes some serious commitment. When he told me he was Joseph I wanted the ground to open and swallow me whole...but I wanted him to come along for the ride. Whilst I can't think of anything more horrifying than playing his pregnant virgin wife, I also can't think of anyone I'd rather be doing it with. His deep penetrating voice skated across my skin, and I pray to god that he didn't notice my physical reaction, because I want him to take me and this seriously.

'Morning.'

I bolt upright, slamming my head against the hard oak headboard.

'Shit, sorry...' He winces.

I slowly take him all in as I soothe the back of my head. He's fully dressed, standing in the doorway, holding a tray laden with food.

'What's this?' I croak, pulling Billy into my arms.

'Peace offering?' He seats himself on the edge of the bed, his t-shirt flexing around his muscles as he passes me two plates.

I frown as I take in the difference between the sandwiches.

'One's for Billy,' he says, forcing a reluctant smile.

'Would that be the one cut into a fish shape?'

'Uh huh.' He rubs the back of his neck and drops his gaze to the floor. 'I'm really sorry, Penny. I didn't mean to make you feel uncomfortable yesterday. I'm really grateful you're doing this for us. I was never holding out for someone else...I just...' He stares out into the hallway. 'I can't talk about it. I wish I could.'

A lump rises to my throat as my own burdening thoughts rush to the forefront of my mind. All I wanted was to forget about Henry and Molly and being here has helped me do that, but whatever is bothering Gabriel, reminds me that I can't hide from the reality of what's happened forever. At some point I'm going to have to face it and I'll have to talk about it too eventually.

'It's okay.' I reach out, placing my hand on his bicep, and he turns and smiles gently. 'You don't have to say anything. For what it's worth, I'm sorry about everything I said yesterday. I went a bit postal. I overreacted. I'd love it if we were friends?'

His brow knits together as he contemplates my proposal.

'Friends sounds good,' he says.

He passes me a glass of orange juice from the tray and as I take a sip my eyes widen from the fresh burst of citrus.

'You weren't wrong though,' Gabriel says, standing to tower above me.

'About what?'

He backs away and leans, arms stretched across the door-frame, and my lips part as I admire the curve of every muscle he has on show.

'You, Penny Hastings, are no one's understudy. You're the lead. The Virgin flippin' Mary. Rehearsals start in an hour.' With a grin plastered across his face he disappears down the stairs.

What the hell have I said yes to.

Chapter Ten

Gabriel

I glance from the wings to where Penny's being given a stern talking to by Helen. She's been a member of this church for longer than I've been alive. Year after year, without fail, she helps my father bring this whole thing together. I can predict every word that comes from her lips, it's like her mantra. Observe your markings, project your voice, remember your cues. I should rescue Penny before she becomes overwhelmed, but the last thing I want to do is crowd her. Friends she said...and friends I think I can manage. It will be hard to forget her reaction to me yesterday, but perhaps it's for the best. When she first arrived, I was adamant we'd keep our distance, but her mere presence has chipped away at my resolve and now we're spending more time together than I dared to imagine.

I can't allow myself to forget that unfortunate circumstances have brought us together and continue to keep us together, but nothing changes the fact that after the nativity we'll both return to our normal lives. Miles apart. It would be stupid to even think about initiating anything, because long distance does not work, and even if it did, there's still this Henry guy, whoever he is, and I can't risk that things there wouldn't rekindle. It's all too unsettling and familiar, and now she's Mary, it's ten times worse.

'Where in heaven did she come from?'

My shoulder jolts forward as I'm nudged heavily by one of the three Wise Men. I don't recognise this one, he must be new.

'Simon, good to meet you. Heard a lot about you, from your dad that is. I'm Mr Frankincense.'

I take one look at the tattoo poking out from his collar and curling around his neck. *Mr Frankenstein more like.*

'Gabriel.' I offer my hand in greeting.

'So, is there anything going on with you and Mary? Beyond the immaculate conception that is.' His laugh echoes across the stage and Penny and Helen abruptly turn in our direction.

'Excuse me?' My eyes narrow.

'Are you an item?'

Is he seriously trying to pick up women at a nativity rehearsal? 'No,' I force out.

'Ah, good, didn't want to step on anyone's sandals.' He laughs again and slaps me on the back. I clench my jaw and bite my tongue. If this wasn't my father's church and this wasn't a member of the congregation, I'd march him so far from this hall that he wouldn't even make it back in time for next Christmas.

'I think I'll introduce myself.' He pushes past and saunters to the centre of the stage. Horror grips me as he takes Penny's hand and raises it to his lips. I've not even been that brazen and we're sharing a damn bed. My fists ball at my sides and my shoulders hunch as tension flows through them. I strain to hear the conversation but all I can focus on is her radiant smile under the brightness of the spotlights. Every so often I catch her gentle laugh and before I can even process what's even going on, she reaches out and squeezes Simon's arm. My heart thunders in my chest as their conversation continues, and I grip tightly to the stage partitioning as she draws her phone from her pocket and passes it to him. *She's giving him her number...I don't even have her number.* Anger simmers in the pit of my stomach, slowly rising and threatening to spill out. There's no way I'm going to watch this play out for the rest of rehearsal. It's time I reminded everyone why I've played Joseph for the last ten years.

Penny

'How can the Son of God be born in a dirty stable?'

'It's okay, Mary. The Lord will provide, and you and the baby will be out of the cold.'

Gabriel stares down at me with an intensity I wasn't expecting for a church nativity. Something runs between us, and it's more than a promise of stable for the night. No, whatever this is, is unspoken and has every one of my nerves on edge. And having an audience of both of his parents and one parishioner doesn't help.

'Very good! Wonderful, what chemistry you two have!' Charles cries from the foot of the stage.

Chemistry? If chemistry means tolerating each other just enough to sleep in the same bed, then sure, we have it by the bucket load. I hoped that my offer of friendship would have called a timely truce, but ever since the rehearsal started, he's been, well...Gabriel.

'I think that everyone else is familiar with the rest of the script. So, tomorrow we'll bring the choir in for one full dress rehearsal before the big night. How does that sound?' Helen adds.

I bounce my head in agreement and glance up at Gabriel for confirmation.

'I'd say some people are too familiar,' he mutters.

'What?' I say, arching my brow.

'Yes, fine, it doesn't bother me. Let's get on with it. The sooner this is all done with the better.'

My cheeks burn with embarrassment as I look between all four of them.

'Gabriel!' Margaret cries.

I gather my script from where it's laid out before me and quickly stand. 'Excuse me.' I push past Gabriel and take the steps to the stage as fast as my legs will carry me. The doors to the hall clatter behind me as I force my way out into the knee-deep snow. As I wade through the fresh coating, which has fallen during rehearsals, I curse myself for believing that I could do this. Who in their right mind takes on the lead in a Christmas nativity for a parish that she isn't even a part of, whilst lodging with a man she barely knows?

Me.

After Henry you'd have thought I'd learnt my lesson about taking men at their word, but oh no. He lied to my face this morning. Friends? Yeah right.

I fling the cottage door open on its hinges and from the corner of my eye I catch Billy dart across the room.

'Billy Bear. I need you.' Without faltering, he rushes to my side. This is friendship, in its truest form right here. Whatever that was back there was laughable.

'Penny!' Gabriel hurtles through the door behind me.

'What?'

'What just happened?' he says breathlessly.

My eyes widen and I release Billy to the ground. Un-fucking-believable.

'You tell me.' I throw my coat to the couch and wobble as I struggle to remove my boots.

He falls silent, his face dropping until his brow knits together.

'Well, I'm waiting?'

His eyes follow me as I move towards the rocking chair. *I don't care how much he loves this bloody seat. I'm claiming it tonight.*

I study him as he forces his tongue fortuitously around his mouth, contemplating his grand explanation. Whatever it is, it better be good.

'Wise man number two,' he says slowly.

'Simon? What about him?' I wrinkle my nose.

'You said you were committed to this nativity, and there you were swapping numbers and being all touchy,' he says, taking one step towards me.

Is he for real right now? 'Why are you watching me?' I hold my hands up. 'In fact, don't bother answering that. If you must know, what you saw was him keying in the closest petrol station so I can refill my car. Which is a damn sight more helpful than you've been.'

His mouth parts, but no words come out. His body visibly relaxes.

'Don't you have anything to say?'

'I'm sorry.'

'Are you? Because this morning I asked you if we could be friends and you said yes and then you call me out on an innocent conversation in front of your parents. It was humiliating, Gabriel. I was starting to think maybe you liked me enough to have me stick around for this nativity, but clearly, I was wrong.'

His chest rises and falls rapidly and whatever emotion he's suppressing, it's fighting to get out. Silence extends out between us and with my last nerve severed, I force my way past him.

'I'm over being treated like this...find yourself another Mary. I'm done.'

'I-I do like you.'

My eyes fall to where his hand has curled around my arm,

stopping me in my tracks. My heart skips its next beat as his grip intensifies and his fingers slide along my upper arm, before moving to tip my chin towards him.

'I do, Penny. I really do.'

'Prove it.'

Chapter Eleven

Penny

His lips crash to mine, his arms surrounding me as he draws my body into his. My feet barely brush the ground as he takes my weight, pulling me deeper into our embrace. *Holy shit.* He moves us blindly backwards until I find myself straddling his lap, desperately fighting for air between kisses.

His hands slide up into my hair and he pulls me roughly from his mouth. 'Is this enough proof for you?'

'Uh huh.' I pant, urgently clawing at his shirt.

My eyes drop to where our bodies meet, and I roll my hips against his growing erection. He stifles a moan and reaches behind his head and lifts his shirt off in one swift movement. I wildly pull at my own clothes, not wanting or daring to break this connection.

The sharp tug of my hair tips my head back and with my neck fully exposed, he drops his mouth, trailing kisses along my jaw, down towards my chest.

My stomach twists in anticipation; I've never known foreplay this frantic. Hands, lips, teeth...grazing against my bare skin. The clasp of my bra pings against my back and in one deft movement he has my breasts in his hands, teasing at my nipples. The explosive sensation has me arching towards him, seeking more.

'Do you have...anything?' I murmur breathlessly into his hair.

His kiss slows, and I clench, bracing myself for the answer.

'Yes...are you sure this is what you want though?'

Relief settles my racing heart and I drag myself from his lap and slowly peel my leggings and underwear off.

With his eyes locked on my face, his throat bobs. 'I'll take that as a yes then.'

'I would.'

He stands towering above me and without even looking fumbles around with his wallet before tossing it to one side. The corners of his mouth curl upwards as he tears the foil packet with his teeth. 'Here,' he says, removing the condom and passing it to me.

I hold it tentatively between my fingertips as he removes his jeans and boxers, kicking them to one side. I drop my gaze, curbing any sign of instant appreciation.

One word. *Blessed.*

I wrap my hand around his length, gripping him firmly, and a short blast of air whistles between his teeth as I roll the condom down.

'You're fucking torturing me, Penny.'

He swiftly turns me to face away from him and falls back to the rocking chair, dragging me on to his body. The tip of his cock brushes against me as I straddle his lap, and as I raise my hips, the chair angles backwards and I blindly reach out to grip his thick, muscular arms to steady myself.

'Gabriel...I don't think—'

'Don't think. Just fuck me. I've got you.'

His legs spread wide underneath me, steadying the sway of the chair, and I drop my head back to his shoulder as I lower my body inch by inch on to his. I sharply inhale as I take all of him, my body moulding perfectly around him, committing to memory his size and shape.

One of his arms wraps protectively around my middle whilst his other hand drops between my legs.

'Mmmm. Feeling my cock disappear inside you is better than anything my imagination has conjured up.'

His hips raise slightly to meet every bounce of my body and the more urgent our thrusts the harder the chair rocks.

'You've been thinking about fucking me?' I pant.

'All. The. Time.'

The slap of our skin against one another echoes through the cottage, and his grip tightens around my waist as a thin layer of sweat breaks out across my chest. I cry out as his teeth graze my neck and his fingers settle into a rhythm against my clit. His timing is impeccable, and my body succumbs willingly with every precise roll of his hips.

We've pushed against each other for days. Strangers, battling our way through the circumstances that have brought us together. It was bound to come to a head, we were doomed from the very beginning. And now I'm going to give in completely, and I don't think I've ever experienced relief like it.

'Gabriel—'

'I know. I won't stop. I couldn't, even if I wanted to...' he grinds out.

My orgasm crashes through me and I gasp for air from the unexpected hit. I knew I was close, but I didn't know it was imminent. Gabriel pulls my body down with one full final thrust and shudders against me. The chair oscillates to a slow stop as he holds me close against him. I turn my head and he drops his chin towards me and captures my lips in one last kiss.

'Satisfied?' he murmurs.

'Very,' I whisper.

Gabriel

When she asked me to prove it, taking her roughly from behind in a rocking chair, rather than the comfort of a soft warm bed, is probably not what she had in mind. She fried my brain and now I'm absolutely fucked. One day away from the nativity and I've fallen dramatically at the last hurdle.

Penny's body twists and her leg slips casually over mine, like it's something we've always done. In reality, we're still strangers sharing a bed, but now we're daring to cross that invisible line. I search out her hand and weave my fingers with her own, and she sighs with contentment, resting her head on my chest.

'Night after night we've navigated the logistics of one bed and when it comes down to it, we have sex on the most awkward piece of furniture ever invented. From now on it's a sex chair not a rocking chair,' she murmurs against my bare skin.

'Don't all women want adventurous sex?' I laugh softly.

Her fingers lock down hard on mine and my body tenses in response.

'Honesty. We just want honesty.'

I swallow hard as things turn serious. 'I don't think I've lied—'

'No, I'm not saying you have... I'm just saying, you know, it's good to be upfront and open so people don't get hurt further down the line. Like if you don't want to be with someone you should say.'

I silently agree. I don't think I've heard a truer word spoken.

'Not that I'm asking for anything from you. After the nativity, we're just going to go back to our own lives, aren't we?' she rushes out.

My stomach flips at the mention of returning to normality, and I know I'd keep us in this Christmas bubble for as long as possible if I could. But if going back to our everyday lives is what she wants, I'm setting myself up to get hurt all over again if I confess my true feelings. I may have surrendered in the face of physical temptation, but protecting my heart is more important.

'Yes, of course, we live so far away from one another,' I say, confirming our position.

'Right.'

Silence consumes the bedroom, giving a final and solemn definition to whatever this was between us. The scratch of claws against the door breaks me from my sobering thoughts and then I remember, if I can give her any part of myself to keep without fear of breaking, it's my honesty.

'Penny...I have lied to you. I'm...not allergic to cats. I'm scared of them.'

'I know,' she whispers.

Her free hand slides up into my hair and she angles my face down towards her. The moonlight peaking through the curtain captures her face perfectly, and she tentatively edges forward before taking my lips in the softest of kisses. And then, as hard as we might want to fight it, we fall back into each other, forgetting everything we've just said.

Chapter Twelve

Penny

The beam of the spotlights glare down heavily, like god himself is shining upon us. Yet after last night, I hope he isn't, because nothing screams fraud like the Virgin Mary having energetic rocking chair sex, followed by slow all-consuming, passionate bed sex.

As I angle up at Gabriel, flashbacks of his body moving against mine ripple through my consciousness. Deep, hard, sinful thrusts...that had no business being administered by the son of a reverend.

'Penny, it's your line,' Gabriel whispers.

'Errr...'

'Penny. Is your mind elsewhere? Do you need a minute?' Margaret calls up from her spot next to Charles.

It's somewhere alright. In the gutter. With your son's cock deep down my thr—

'Why don't we take a break?' Gabriel blurts out, pulling me to my feet.

'Fine,' Charles huffs. 'Just five though, the choir will be here in a minute.'

My feet barely touch the ground as Gabriel whisks me into the wings. My back hits the stage partitioning with a thud as he crowds me unexpectedly.

'You're giving us away...one eye fuck at a time.'

'What? No, I'm n—'

His lips take mine with an intense, mesmerising kiss. If this is supposed to help me remember lines, he's going to have to think of something else.

He pulls back quickly, his eyes rapidly darting across my face. 'You know...seeing you in this veil...in this gown...it's a turn-on.'

A small laugh escapes my lips, and he places a finger to my mouth to silence me.

'Shhh, they'll hear you. This is supposed to be a quick five minutes.' His hand traces along the outline of my body and inch by inch the costume material sweeps up my thigh, until his fingers connect with my skin.

I hold my breath, pinning my eyes closed as I wait for his touch exactly where I need it.

'Open your eyes.' My eyelids flutter, and there he is inches from my face, breathing heavily, staring with a burning intensity as he slips one finger, followed by a second, inside me. He's slow at first and I'm so focused on the movement that I forget I'm even in the church hall.

'Gabriel...' I warn as his touch quickens against me, 'anyone could see us.'

'No one will come back here. Trust me.'

'Uncle Gabriel...' The twins' high-pitched squeal echoes through the hall and his hand stills against me.

Worst. Timing. Ever.

'You've got to be kidding me,' he hisses against my throat as he peppers me with light kisses. He steps away and readjusts himself as I return my costume to a more orderly fashion.

'There you are!' they cry, appearing from the darkness.

'Yes. There you both are...' he forces out.

'Come see, come see, Daddy has brought a real tree, but it's too big to get through the door!'

Gabriel throws me disgruntled look and follows the girls out into the hall. This screams disaster.

Gabriel

The last bars of 'Joy to the World' ring around the hall and a peaceful silence surrounds the cast. This is the best the production has looked in years and I can't deny that's down to the excitement of a stranger playing Mary. There's a buzz throughout the hall, and if the whisperings I catch are to be believed, then there's no doubt in everyone's mind that Penny's best Virgin Mary we've ever had, whether she remembers her lines or not.

'You lied to me the other day.'

My back stiffens at the sound of a familiar voice. I turn and there he is, practically squaring up to me.

'Simon...'

'Don't Simon me. I asked if anything was going on between you and Penny and you said no. And it quite clearly is, she can barely keep her eyes off you.'

I shrug in response. There's no way I'm sharing my personal business with him. 'She's Mary, I'm Joseph, she's only supposed to have eyes for me. A little frankincense isn't going to change that...or petroleum for that matter.'

'Huh. I see, threatened, are you?'

I gaze across the hall, taking in Penny as she engages with some of the choir and fellow cast. Just seeing her immerse herself in everything, reminds me how long it's been since I've been able to share this moment with someone special. 'Not at all. Why would I be?' I say confidently, turning back towards Simon.

'Because you and Mary don't have the best track record, maybe you think after the nativity's up she's going to run off with someone else like Olivia did all those years ago.'

I step forward, closing the last of the gap between us. Rage flares inside me at the very mention of her name.

'Who's been talking? Was it Helen? Actually, do you know what, forget it,' I say, holding both hands up in defence. 'Let's get one thing clear, Simon. Penny's nothing like Olivia and there isn't anyone for her to be running off with, she's single. Secondly, nothing is going on.'

'Sure, right. You keep telling yourself that.'

From the corner of my eye, I spot Penny break away and start to move towards us.

I take his costume in a firm grip and twist the material until we're eye to eye. 'If I hear one more—'

'Gabriel, I've left you a present outside the cottage,' Adam says, appearing from behind me.

I release my grasp on Simon's shirt and shoot him a look, causing him to back away slowly and silently.

'I don't want a bloody present. What is it?'

'Something for you and Penny.'

'Oooh, what is it?' Penny asks, finally joining us.

'Ahh, you'll find out when you go back home, all I'll say is that the cat will love it!'

A worried expression shoots across her face. Billy loves three things. Penny, sleep and food. A sense of dread fills me. I wanted a quiet night in with her, no drama, no fuss.

'Ah, would you look at that!' Adam exclaims, arms stretched

wide in front of the ridiculously large tree he's erected right by the stage. 'Isn't she a beauty?'

This is why he shouldn't be left in charge of anything, especially nativity decorations. 'We'll be finding pine needles this time next Christmas.'

Adam nudges Penny in the side and winks at me and even though he's my brother, all my defences kick in. 'For heaven's sake, take him home, would you, and try and instil some Christmas spirit into him.'

She laughs quietly and her gentle smile softens my hardened exterior. If anyone can break down my walls and bring some Christmas joy back into my life, it's her.

Chapter Thirteen

Gabriel

Fucking fantastic.

I stare at the Norway spruce propped against the outside of the cottage. Penny's eyes widen, sparkling at the prospect.

'Billy will love this!'

'Of course, he will, the tree will be on the floor by the morning, pine needles, baubles, scattered everywhere. Cats and Christmas trees do not mix.'

Her eyes roll as she manoeuvres past the branches into the cottage. I glance back and forth a few times before hoisting the trunk over my shoulder. 'I suppose I'm bringing this in then, am I?'

'You'd suppose correct!' she calls over her shoulder, whilst cradling Billy.

I struggle through the doorway and swing the tree from left to right as I decide upon the perfect location. Never having had a tree here before, there's no customary place.

'Where do you want it?'

'Where do *you* want it?' She wiggles her eyebrows at me, placing Billy to the floor.

'The tree, Penny. This is heavy.'

She points to the right of the fireplace and it's a good a spot as any. The trunk hits the ground with a thud, and I step back, my forehead creasing as the top branches graze the ceiling. *For Christ's sake Adam.*

'You'll need to chop a bit off.'

My eyes widen and I shake my head. 'Two and a half orgasms and you think you know it all, don't you?'

Her teeth sink into her bottom lip, and she smiles, thrusting a pile of boxes towards me.

'Oh...what are they?' I sigh.

'They're from your mum and she left a note. It says, *Penny and Gabriel, here are some tree decorations, mulled wine and board games for you now Penny's staying for Christmas...*' She slows as she looks up from the paper. Staying one more day for the nativity is one thing but beyond that is something we haven't discussed.

'Are you staying?' I hold my breath as I wait for a response. If she stays after the nativity, then it will be Christmas Day and she'll be pushed to find a petrol station around here open on December the twenty-fifth.

'Do you want us to?'

My eyes flick to the long-haired creature at her feet and he purrs heavily as he brushes against her legs. I fight against the smile threatening to break and nod casually. 'I guess I could tolerate you both for an extra day.'

'I'll call my parents then...' she whispers.

Penny

Nothing beats the scent of a real Christmas tree. Henry and I only ever had a plastic one, because he said why would he go out to buy a new one every year when he could climb into the attic and retrieve it instead.

'Mum and Dad weren't back from the airport, so I left a message,' I call, as I pour the last of the mulled wine into our glasses.

'Do you think they'll be worried?' he asks, at the same time stepping back to admire his handy work.

'No, I'm a grown woman.'

'So, star or angel?' he says, waving both decorations towards me.

'Angel...definitely angel Gabriel.' I hiccup and laugh simultaneously.

'Very funny,' he says, pulling me towards him and holding my body firmly in front of his. 'Here, you do the honours.'

He lifts me slightly and I take the angel from him and place it proudly on the top.

'Perfect.' His breath is warm against my skin and his lips graze against my ear before travelling down to my neck. I nuzzle into his touch as his kiss intensifies. 'Bed?'

'No rocking chair tonight?'

He chuckles and the sensation vibrates against me, causing me to break out in the biggest smile I've had in months.

'No, I want you naked and underneath me. In fact, I need it.'

'Is that any way to be speaking to your virgin wife?' I bite my lip as I await his response.

Without breaking our connection, he navigates us towards the stairs, and my stomach swirls as he takes control. 'You're forgetting, I've seen the way you fuck, there's nothing virginal about it.'

The bedroom is warmed from the rising heat from the fireplace and as soon as Gabriel kicks the door shut behind us, we're tearing the clothes from each other's bodies. He fists at the duvet, tearing it from the bed, leaving nothing but the sheet and pillows.

'What are you doing?'

'Tonight, there's nothing between us, we've spent too many nights in this bed as strangers. Tonight, when I'm finished with you, you'll fall asleep with me wrapped around you, not a duvet, not a wall of pillows, nothing.'

'And tomorrow?' I murmur against his lips as I drag him backwards.

'I plan to do it all again.'

He drops to his knees and with only my underwear left, he hooks his fingers into the elastic and peels them down until they pool around my ankles.

'Absolute heaven,' he says, inhaling deeply.

His hands mirror each other as they trail along the backs of my legs. With the gentlest of pushes, I fall back, and he crawls over me, boxing me in. He peppers kisses between my breasts, straight down to my naval, and the closer he gets to my sex the tighter my body clenches in anticipation.

'I left you on the edge earlier. Time to put things right...' His tongue swirls once around my clit and my back arches high from the bed. His large hands grasp at my thighs, pushing them back against the mattress, and it's the most exposed I've been with a man ever.

As I glance down, his eyes flick up and he pulls back to where I can see his glistening smile.

'You're so ready for this, aren't you? I can taste it.'

My mouth falls open and no words come out, but I know what I want. I reach out to the bedside in search of the condom box we discarded there last night. I pull him up along my body and his tongue dips between my lips in the most tender of kisses, teasing and caressing in a way I've never experienced. The familiar ache tightens in my core and I clench, trying to hold on to it for just that little bit longer. Our bodies slide against one another, my soft curves moulding into his toned muscles, like the missing piece of a jigsaw. He silently rolls the condom on, and his arms surround me. Raising his body up high over mine, his legs spread wide between my own, pinning me against the mattress.

Our eyes meet and amid our desperation a sense of calm passes between us.

My insides ripple as Gabriel sinks into me in one smooth hard thrust. Dropping his head next to mine, a strangled moan slips through the air.

'God, so good, Penny.'

I brace my body as his thrusts pick up the pace and fall deep, hitting that spot inside that only someone with skill could find. He slips his arms under my legs, raising them towards my shoulders, causing my eyes to roll back. I desperately claw at the sheets to ground myself, to bring me back to here and now, to remind myself that this is really happening. He might be named after an angel, but he fucks like the devil.

Wicked, unforgiving, and unrepentant.

Our sweat-covered bodies struggle against one another, fighting for control.

'Don't chase it, let me give this to you,' he murmurs softly. 'I can wait for you.'

'You can?' I heave breathlessly.

His hand slips to where our bodies meet, massaging me on every timed thrust. *Oh god, that will do it.*

'And all this time I thought you hated it.'

'What?' he pants.

'Sleeping in the same bed as me.' *Oh god.*

He raises his hands to the headboard, and I know now I'm definitely in for it.

'I loved.' Slam.

'Every.' Slam.

'Last.' Slam.

'Second.'

Holy... 'Gabriel...'

He drops his forehead to mine. 'I know, Pen.'

I hurtle into a blinding orgasm that rips through me from the inside out. He surrounds me in every way, holding me close. The subtle twitch of his body signals his own climax, that confirms that he did one hundred per cent wait for me. Time blurs as we lose ourselves in a deep, unhurried kiss, the perfect end to the most incredible sex I've ever had. Rocking chair included.

As he moves from my body, he takes me with him as he rolls on to his side, his arm wrapped protectively around me, in exactly the way he said he would.

He called me Pen. Strangers don't call me that. People who know me do – people who love me.

Chapter Fourteen

Penny

We've had the most perfect morning, after the most perfect evening, and with the nativity only hours away, my nerves are starting to show.

'Please stop pacing. You'll be fine. In fact, you'll be more than fine, you'll be the best Mary ever,' Gabriel pleads, staring up from his sprawled-out position on the couch. With his white t-shirt and grey joggers, he looks positively delicious, and I can't believe I missed out on three days and nights of sampling the delights of what that body has to offer.

I repeat his words over in my head and that's when yesterday's conversation comes flooding back to me. After the excitement of the real tree and the mulled wine and the orgasms... plural, I completely forgot I'd even overheard any of the conversation he had with Simon.

'Who's Olivia?' I blurt out without hesitation.

Gabriel bolts upright and grips the edge of the couch. Whoever she is...she's important if she evokes this reaction.

'Sorry, I—'

'No. Honesty, right?'

Oh god. My stomach rolls. *Who is she?* I nod quickly, praying we can get this conversation over with. If there is someone else, I think I'll need another mini break to get over it. And if so, I'm taking the next one at a nunnery.

'She...she's my ex-girlfriend. We were each other's first everything.'

I sink down on to the couch next to him. He stares straight ahead, unable and unwilling to look me in the eye. He inhales and continues.

'She was my first heartbreak. My only heartbreak to be fair. But I suppose – and this is why you've heard her name – she was my first Mary.'

'Oh...'

'Yes. Oh,' he says, slouching back against the cushions.

'And what happened?'

'Well...we played Joseph and Mary for the first time when we were seventeen and then again when we were eighteen, but by the time we'd turned nineteen we'd both been away at separate universities for a term and I couldn't wait to get back to here, to the nativity...to her.' He pauses in reflection and laughs quietly. 'I suppose looking back I knew something wasn't right, but I ignored it, you know. Like deep down I knew something was going on, but I wasn't brave enough to confront her. She seemed different, distant almost. She blamed it on the nativity, but she knew the script like the back of her hand. Anyway, after the choir rang out their final verse, she turned to me and told me she had met someone else and was leaving to go back to university to be with him for Christmas.'

'Oh my god.'

'Yeah...so, that's Olivia, and that's why I like to be alone... did like to be alone.'

'Has there been anyone else?'

'Nothing ever serious enough to risk me getting my heart broken again. You're lucky the only thing Henry left you with was this mini break.'

I roll my lips, stifling my confession. This isn't about me, it's about Gabriel. When the time's right I'll tell him about my failed engagement and cancelled wedding, but for now I need to make sure that this nativity is best one since Olivia.

'And what a mini break it's been.'

He brushes the hair back from my face and smiles. 'I'm one lucky carpenter.'

Leaning forward, I brush my lips against his. 'I'm one lucky virgin.'

❄

The church hall is quiet. With only an hour until the nativity, it's the calm before the storm. Monty's loud bray echoes along the corridor, and I smile to myself, puffing out a burst of air as I fan my face.

'Helen, I wish we'd tried this on sooner.' I peer down as she rustles around under my gown. I must be some kind of idiot because I thought I was going to shove a jumper under my shirt, like in school, but oh no, full on prosthetic bump that no one warned me about.

'Nearly there,' her muffled voice sounds from beneath me.

'How are things coming along?' Gabriel asks, placing a hand in the small of my back.

'Contractions are about five minutes apart, still got a while.'

'Huh. Good one.' Helen snorts, pulling herself to her feet and pushing her glasses back into place. 'Right, I'll leave you both to it. An hour until showtime, try and relax.' As she wanders off, Gabriel drops his mouth next to my ear.

'I know something that might relax you...'

I swat him playfully and peer out to the empty hall. In an hour's time this will be full to the rafters, and I can't lie, I'm absolutely terrified. Still, it's not like I know anyone.

'You'll be amazing, Pen.'

'I like it when you call me that.' I beam up at him.

'I like calling you it.' He drops his head until his nose brushes mine and, in this moment, there's nowhere else I'd rather be.

'I'm sorry, the doors don't open for the audience for another forty minutes,' I hear Helen shout across the hall.

Gabriel peers around the stage partitioning and frowns. 'That's odd.'

'What is?' I nip his neck lightly with a claiming kiss.

'I don't recognise him. Never seen him before.'

The conversation quietens and it's not until I catch the rumble of the stage steps that I really pay attention.

'Erm, Penny...' Helen calls.

I glance up at Gabriel and he smiles, linking his fingers with mine, and in a show of unity, we step out from the shadows.

'Yes, Helen?'

Her eyes drop to our hands and quickly back up to my face and her clipboard waves mindlessly behind her. 'There's a man here to see you. He says he's your fiancé.'

Gabriel's body stiffens beside me, and his hand falls from mine.

'What? No, there must be some mistake. I'm—'

'Penny?' Henry's voice travels from the darkness and I freeze. *This can't be happening*. 'Penny, is that you?' He laughs and steps into the periphery of the stage lighting, clasping a bunch of flowers in one hand and a petrol can in the other.

'W-what are you doing here?' I force out.

'Oh boy, it's true,' Helen mutters.

'What no!' I cry, turning towards a numb looking Gabriel.

'Gabriel, this isn't what it looks like. We're not...I mean we were, but...'

I tear the veil from my head and shake it at Henry. 'What do you want? Who sent you?'

'Your parents. You left them some garbled message about staying in a cottage with some stranger and you had no petrol.'

'And they sent you?'

He hunches his shoulders and holds out the bouquet. 'They want us to be together. Who else would they send?'

'Oh, I don't know, anyone but the man who cheated on me with my best friend, moving her into our flat and kicking me out,' I cry, throwing my hands in the air.

'They don't know though, do they? You never told them.'

My body shakes from the anger building inside. I can't believe that he's here and he has the audacity to still use the word fiancé. 'No, I never told them. It's humiliating and besides, I only found out a few days ago and they were away.'

Gabriel stands quietly, staring blankly out into the empty hall.

'Molly was a mistake. You don't have to live with someone for long to know if they're right for you or not.'

My heart flutters. *He's right...you don't.*

'It's not too late, Penny, we can still get married tomorrow, like we planned. Come on, you and me, like you always wanted.'

'Tomorrow? You were getting married...tomorrow?' Gabriel slowly turns towards me and his haunted eyes hold mine.

I nod slowly. 'But we're over. He hasn't been my fiancé for months.'

'You should have told me,' he says through gritted teeth. 'Honesty is all you want, remember? I opened up to you this morning, it was your perfect opportunity.'

'Gabriel, please.' Panic rises inside me, and I don't care that

Helen and Henry are watching on. 'This, this means something, doesn't it?' I gesture between us.

Gabriel swallows hard and forces himself to look away.

'You were so sure you had me figured out when I arrived and the reasons why I was here alone, and...well, I was too embarrassed to admit the truth.'

'Oh, so this is my fault, is it?' He seethes.

'Look, is there something I should know?' Henry butts in.

Silence swirls between us. Henry doesn't deserve a moment of my wasted breath. What's between me and Gabriel is our business and no one else's.

'No. Nothing,' Gabriel says finally.

Nothing?

'What's going on?' Charles interjects as he storms the stage steps, closely followed by Margaret, Adam and the twins.

'Penny's fiancé is here. They're getting married tomorrow,' Helen rushes out.

'No! We're not!'

Gabriel weaves between us all, pulling desperately at his costume.

'Gabriel, wait, this is a huge misunderstanding.'

He stops and turns, taking us all in one by one, and shakes his head. 'No, I understand, but this has been a mistake.'

My heart free falls as he walks away, tearing at his tunic. I rush forward, desperate to go to him, but Margaret sweeps in and ushers me away. Tears stain my cheeks and everything blurs. We go on stage in less than an hour, but right now, more than the nativity hangs in the balance.

Chapter Fifteen

Gabriel

This costume is suffocating. I sweep layers upon layers of material over my head as I charge towards the cottage. *Fiancé?* I can't believe it. Actually, I can. Because of course someone as amazing as Penny has been snapped up. My chest hurts, constricted by the similarities between my present and past circumstances.

She'll leave.

After the nativity, she'll go, the same as Olivia, and I'll let her because I… Because that's the right thing to do.

I slam the door forcefully in my wake and sink into the rocking chair, reaching for the bottle of whiskey conveniently placed on the side table. I never drink before a performance, but something tells me I'm going to need to take the edge off this one.

'You…' I murmur as Billy stalks into view. 'This is all your fault.' I point at him as I pour one solitary measure. 'If it wasn't for you accosting me on that first night, I wouldn't have ended up in bed with her and I wouldn't be sat here like this right now.'

Meep.

What even is that noise? It's not a purr, it's not a meow, yet it's all I've heard for days. It's like he's having a conversation. He jumps from the couch, landing directly at my feet. His eyes twitch back and forth, and he rears up, and my body stills. 'No, don't you even—'

He lands in my lap and promptly sits. *Meep.*

'What do you want?' I sigh.

His paws pad repeatedly against my chest, and I don't even flinch. With one swipe of a well-sharpened claw, he could sever an artery and that would be my lot. I've lived a good life and what a way to go. He edges closer and the vibration of his purr is almost soothing, and then in a strange and unexpected gesture, he nudges his head against mine. Not once, but twice, and I'll be damned if this cat isn't giving me his blessing. 'I think I love her, Billy.'

I drop my head in despair; I'm clearly bordering on insanity because after a matter of days I think I'm in love, and two...I'm talking to a cat. Her ex may be a complete dick, but he was right about one thing, you don't have to live with someone long to know if they're right for you. Because she was right from the beginning, I was the idiot. How am I supposed to compete with the kind of history she has with Henry though.

Meep. I ruffle the long hair around his neck and hold his beady little stare. 'Yeah, but I think I should probably let her go.'

I lower him to the floor and stand, downing the remainder of the amber liquid in my glass. I scrub my hand across my face and shake out all four limbs. I need to breathe some life back into me if I'm going to make it through the next hour. I force the costume back over my head and pull open the cottage door, and there Penny stands illuminated by the glow of the moon, looking every inch the virgin.

'Can we talk?'

Her face is damp, her eyes puffy, and regret hits me that I walked out rather than hear her out. On the face of it we're still strangers, but I've shared more with her in the last few days than I have with anyone in years. Listening to what she has to say is the least I can give her. I glance briefly at my phone and my eyes widen. 'We don't have time. We're on stage in ten minutes.'

'After then?'

I nod stoically, pulling the door closed behind me, and I guide her along the path.

We walk briskly in silence and every so often I cast my eyes to the darkened December sky, and it suddenly hits me that for too many Christmases now, I've looked at these stars alone. I glance across at Penny and she smiles apprehensively and a small part of me regains some hope.

On the approach to the hall, the double doors swing open, and Henry stops, hands firmly on his hips.

'Where the hell have you been? I've been looking everywhere for you. Come on, let's get going.' He points towards her.

We grind to an abrupt halt and instinct has me reaching out to Penny, curling my hand protectively around her forearm.

'I've got a nativity to perform in and even if I didn't, I'm not going anywhere with you, especially up the aisle tomorrow, so crawl back to Molly. You've already ruined my year, I'm not letting you have my Christmas.'

'So, what, you're staying here with him and playing little donkey?' Henry laughs, gesturing towards me. 'He doesn't want you, Pen. What was it you said, mate...a mistake, wasn't it?' He steps towards her and drops his voice to almost a whisper. 'I'm the only one who'll have you.'

The anger that's been building inside me for the last hour

begins to spiral and I force my hand between them, pushing him back.

'She said she isn't going anywhere with you. Do you understand English, or do you need a translator?'

He huffs out a breath and glances up at me. 'Look, no offence, but I don't know you and neither does Penny, how could she after a few days. You should stay out of things that don't concern you.'

My eyes flick to Penny and for the first time in days I see the same hurt that was present when she arrived. A hurt which slowly over our time together has been replaced by something new. That perhaps I've helped her to forget.

'Gabriel, I just want to get inside,' she pleads.

I guide her body towards mine and Henry looks on in disbelief. 'You can't be serious.'

My last nerve snaps and I turn, holding Penny protectively behind me.

'I could ask you the same thing...cheating on her, on anyone for that matter, but especially her! You must be out of your god damn mind.' I turn back and as we're ushering ourselves into the warm, his voice rings out one last time.

'I'm taking the cat then.'

Penny stops dead, fear emanating from her body. She turns in my arms, and I hold her back. 'I've got this. You go.'

Her eyes well as she fights the onslaught of tears. I wait until she's out of sight and roll the sleeves of my costume up as far as they will go. I pick up my pace as I stalk towards him, and he hastily backs away.

'Go near that cat and you'll be drinking your Christmas dinner through a straw.'

'Kiss your mother with that mouth, do you...Gabriel?'

I pause for a second as I contemplate being the bigger man, but where's the fun in that?

I pull him towards me by the lapels of his jacket and he contorts uncomfortably. I lower my voice to a whisper so that what passes between us, will be imprinted on his lowlife cheating brain forever.

'No, but I tongue fucked Penny with it. Merry Christmas.'

I wrench the petrol can from his hand and back away as he looks on in shock. I pause as I reach the doors to the hall and place the can by the entrance. I'll fill her car for her...she doesn't need anyone else.

Chapter Sixteen

Penny

Low chatter vibrates through the hall and part of me is glad I didn't witness the audience arrive, as I'm not sure my nerves could have taken it.

'Oh, thank goodness you're back, Charles was about to have a meltdown,' Margaret says with relief as she repositions my veil. 'Where's Gabriel?' She stills, looking across my shoulder. 'You did speak to him?'

'Well, sort of, I found him, but we—'

'Where is he?' Charles hisses, waving from the erratically from the other side of the stage.

Gabriel looms behind him, planting both firm hands on his shoulders, and Charles visibly relaxes, tipping his head back and mouthing 'thank you' to the heavens.

'Right, curtain in two minutes.' Helen rushes past in a whirlwind.

Gabriel and I stand feet apart as the remaining cast mill around us getting into position. My heart beats heavily in my chest and a lump rises to my throat. I've memorised every word that's about to leave my mouth over the next thirty minutes, but what I'm going to say after, I don't get a rehearsal for. I only get one chance to explain what he means to me, to prove that I'd spend all my Christmases with him if I could. I smile hopefully, praying he'll give me a sign that will get me through the next half hour, but as the curtain raises and the lights dim, only time will tell if there's still a place for me at the cottage when the night is over.

❄

The voices of the choir soften as the last chords of 'O Little Town of Bethlehem' ring out. Gabriel's hand drops to the small of my back as he guides me across the stage, whilst keeping a strong grip on Monty's reigns.

'My wife is about to give birth and we need a place to stay.' His eyes hold mine the whole time as we await the innkeeper's reply.

'There are no rooms left, can't you see how crowded we are?'

There's only one bed. And after today will he even share it with me?

Seconds pass and as I glance out to a sea of expectant faces, I remember this is not my story I'm telling.

'Please...help. I need somewhere to have my child.'

'There are stables nearby. You can find shelter there,' the innkeeper replies.

Gabriel releases a relieved breath and as we fulfil the next lines, the light shifts and we move to the final scene. As I lower myself gingerly to the ground, surrounded by bales of hay, I try to forget that over a hundred people sit before us and instead focus on the one person who really matters. I deliver my final line, and I close my eyes to collect my thoughts as the play continues around me. The Wise Men pass across the stage, bearing their gifts, and the narrator reminds us all why we are here and why we still tell this story. The lone male tenor of the choir breaks out into 'O Holy Night' and the rest of the cast join us on stage. Gabriel rests his hand on my shoulder and squeezes it comfortingly. I know this wasn't in the script and dare to hope that it's a silent message – that everything's going to be okay.

The final song starts and we all make our way into the wings to be greeted by Margaret and Charles.

'What a triumph! Penny you were magnificent.' Reverend Harris pulls me into an embrace, and everyone looks on, beaming from ear to ear.

'This was the best nativity in years. The audience were whispering about it. Penny, so many children want their photo with you, please, will you?'

I turn to Gabriel, and he nods towards the hall. 'My mother's right, Pen, you should go.'

'But—'

'No buts, go. It means so much to people. You were wonderful.'

I promised I was committed, but right now I've never been more reluctant. 'Okay.' I nod.

Margaret holds out her hand and I accept it graciously. As my body brushes past Gabriel, he stills and the overwhelming urge to put things right eats me up. 'I'm sorry...'

'It doesn't matter anymore. Go,' he says, gesturing towards Margaret.

My stomach sinks as we walk away and drops even further when I see the queue of parishioners lining up in the hall with their camera phones at the ready. I shake my head in disbelief. Margaret squeezes my hand and releases me towards the crowd, and I turn in panic.

'I-I didn't sign up for this?'

Her brows raise and she smiles mischievously. 'You'll never forget the moment you said yes to the angel Gabriel, will you?'

Gabriel

As the rest of the cast quietly disperse to celebrate backstage, I stand in the shadows, rooted to the spot in awe. That bloody donkey has been the star attraction for years, but no one gives two shits about him now. She's new, fresh faced, exactly what this nativity needed. Exactly what I needed. I shudder as I think back to my offer of rearranging Henry's smile. I've never threatened anyone like that, but then I've never had the guts to fight for someone before. I've just let them go. This time there's so much more at stake. *What if he didn't leave, what if he did take Billy?* A wave of nausea hits me. It's one thing letting the cat escape onto the roof, but inadvertently handing over custody due to irrational behaviour, that's something else entirely. His expression as I walked away was nothing short of incredulous but hearing that your ex-fiancée had another man's head between her legs is bound to strike a nerve or two. Panic hits me hard. *Shit.* I need to check on the damn cat. I frantically search for my pile of clothes and tear my tunic over my head. The chill in the air bites at my bare skin and I'd give anything to be back in the warmth of the cottage with Penny right now.

Where the hell is my t-shirt?

'Gabriel?'

I spin on the spot, with no regard for the woman that's about to face me and my naked torso. 'Yes, what—'

No.

'Hi, Gabriel.'

I still as I'm transported back to another time. A time that I've tried so hard to forget.

'Olivia...what are you doing here?'

She points absentmindedly and shifts on the spot, clearly as uncomfortable about the situation we find ourselves in as I am. 'I was just passing and I... You look well.'

I clutch the tunic to my chest, like saving my scrap of modesty will make this situation better. 'Yeah, I'm good. You?'

'Yeah, good.'

We both nod, unable to look one another in the eye, years of pent-up emotions threatening to spill out between us.

'I'm not stopping. I'm visiting my parents. They usually come to me, but my circumstances have changed and well, I'm staying with them this year.'

I suck in a burst of much needed air as I digest the information. *She's telling me she's single.* Any other year it may have been welcome news, but I need to fight for my future not fawn over my past.

'As long as you're surrounded by the right people that's all that matters, isn't it?'

Her eyes glisten and despite the heartbreak I suffered at her hands, I can't help but feel some compassion.

'I'm so sorry, Gabriel. I treated you so badly.' Her bottom lip quivers as she spills out her apology.

'It was a long time ago now.'

'It still feels like yesterday to me.' She sniffs.

That's the thing about time, when you have lots of it on your hands it goes slowly, but when you're in a hurry, there's not enough of it. Like now.

'Look, Liv, I'm glad you're well and I really appreciate the apology. But I—'

'It's Mary.'

My brow creases. 'What is?'

'Why you're so happy. I saw you up there with her. I know that nativity script, and you for that matter, and nowhere does it say that Joseph looks longingly at Mary, shooting daggers at any member of the ensemble that dares to get too close.'

'Shit. Was I that obvious?'

Olivia laughs softly and sways from side to side, swinging her bag playfully. 'Yeah, just a little,' she says, pinching her fingers together.

I toss the tunic to one side and pick up my crumpled t-shirt. 'Fuck.' I tip my head back with a growl.

'Not good?' she questions.

I scrub my palm across my face. 'I don't know, she's literally just out of a serious relationship that I only found out about today, and if I'd have known, I might have exercised a bit more caution. It's taken me a long time to find someone and now...I'm worried.'

'In case history repeats itself?'

I nod solemnly.

'Do you want to know what I think?'

'I shouldn't...but yes.'

'You need to stop punishing yourself and everyone else for what I did. Just because I left you with horrible memories of being in love at Christmas, doesn't mean that you should continue to suffer. If she's the one...fight for her.'

I wrinkle my nose, scrunching my face tightly. 'I threatened to put her ex on a liquid diet.'

She snorts loudly and covers her face. 'Oh. Where was this Gabriel all those years ago?'

I shrug, giving her a half-hearted smile. 'Thanks, Liv.'

She steps towards me and loops her arms around my waist and presses her head against my chest. My body goes rigid as I graciously accept her goodbye, and the sensation it evokes is everything I need to prove to myself that there's only one woman I need in my arms.

'Come on, let me walk you out.'

Chapter Seventeen

Penny

'One more photo. With the donkey.'

I force a smile as I stand positioned next to Monty and half of this woman's extended family.

'Thank you, you've been wonderful. You and Joseph make a lovely couple.'

I open my mouth to explain, but I don't think anyone cares about the intricate technicalities of my and Gabriel's situation.

'A lovely couple indeed,' Margaret repeats, sidling up to me.

I laugh nervously as the blush of embarrassment creeps over my cheeks. 'Come, let's get you backstage. I think my son is waiting for you.'

My feet are like lead weights pinning me in place. What if this doesn't go to plan? What if all of that with Henry was for show, to save face? And the heated stares that followed throughout the nativity were anger not desire.

'I know he's a closed book, but you've brought him out of his shell, he's been like my old Gabriel again.'

'How did you—'

'Mother's intuition.' She smiles, tapping her nose. As we reach the foot of the stage, the twins come hurtling towards us, followed by an exhausted looking Adam.

'Girls! Stop running!'

'Sorry, Nanny.'

They each take a hand, prising my fingers open, and start to drag me away. 'You need to come say goodbye to Monty.'

I inwardly groan. I've spent too much time with this flipping donkey tonight, there's only one animal I want to get back to and that's my Billy. I repeat Henry's words over in my head. *I'm taking the cat then.* Gabriel said he'd handle it...but this is the same man who's terrified of cats and only a matter of days ago was prepared to leave him on a roof. If he truly holds a grudge for me keeping quiet about being engaged, then letting Billy go would be the way to level the playing field. The girls squeal as we rush through the foyer. I glance down at my current attire and I can't believe I've spent half the day dressed as the Virgin Mary, but with my clothes backstage, I won't have time to change before I wave off our four-legged friend.

'Penny, hurry,' they cry as they drag me along.

'Girls, you go ahead, I'll be right behind you.' I release both of their hands, allowing them to descend upon Monty and his handler. I grind to a breathless halt, doubling over, gripping my knees. Today has really taken it out of me and I want nothing more than to crawl into bed with Gabriel and fall asleep and forget that the first half of the day even happened.

'Penny!' the girls hiss with a whisper.

I still as I look up at the two figures on the edge of the common, half shielded by a huge 4x4 that I've not seen parked here before.

And then, they shift. It's Gabriel and a woman I don't remember from the parish or the nativity.

He glances down, hunched over, hands deep in his pockets, and she stares up at him for the longest time before reaching out, leaning up and placing a kiss on his cheek. My stomach tightens as I hold my breath. This is nothing. It's platonic. I'd know if there was someone else. Wouldn't I?

He wraps his arms around her and my heart thunders in my chest. *No.*

The doors of the hall rattle loudly behind me and I turn to find Adam scouring the scene before him.

'Ahhh, there they are, the bloody rascals,' he says, pointing at the twins.

'Adam?'

'Yeah?' He pauses and turns to face me.

'Do you know who that is?'

'Bloody hell. Olivia Burton, not seen her in years,' Adam says in disbelief, shaking his head. 'The one that got away.'

My eyes flutter closed and suddenly I'm free falling with no one to reach out and stop me. He said it didn't matter anymore, and now I know why. It was never going to be anything beyond tonight; he may have said I was the lead, but now I can see that I'm always going to be the understudy.

I turn back to face the hall and my eyes drop to the can of petrol, waiting like some kind of Christmas miracle. I stare down at my costume once more and I'm torn; if I want to avoid being let down gently, I need to breeze out of here in the same way I arrived, quickly and unexpectedly.

❄

The cottage is roasting when I step inside, and I'm immediately greeted by Billy having a leisurely rock in the sex chair.

'Come on, Bill, we don't have time for that, we're going.'

He drags his head up, eyeballing me with contempt. 'Yes, I

know you're comfy, I'm sorry, but you need to get in the cat carrier.'

I fly up the stairs and the bedroom door knocks against the wall with a bang. Dropping to my knees, I drag my luggage from underneath the bed and throw every last piece of clothing I can lay my hands on inside. I pause for a moment, if only to analyse my irrational behaviour. I can't have my heartbroken twice this year, and if I learnt anything from the Henry situation, it's that I shouldn't stick around in the hope that Gabriel might change his mind.

My hands grip our crumpled sheets as I pull myself to my feet, and a twinge of sadness hits that we only crossed from strangers to lovers for the briefest of moments. It would never have worked though, Gabriel said it himself, we live so far away from one another, and he knows better than most that long distance only spells disaster. I bump my luggage down the staircase for speed and find Billy waiting expectantly for me at the bottom.

'Right, come here, we don't have time for judgement.' I lift him and for the first time ever he fights me, clawing desperately, avoiding the carrier at all costs. 'Billy, please we don't have time for this. We can't stay here anymore.' I click the door closed as he finally relents, and I hurry to put him in the car. I collect my luggage and hesitate by the door. *Should I leave a note?* It does seem a little pointless when I'm trying to abscond undetected. It's not like we're going to keep in touch, is it? My line of sight shifts to the sex rocking chair, and my parting gesture hits me. Taking the veil from my head I fold it once and lay it neatly on the seat. We may have only had this Christmas, but he'll never sit in this chair again without remembering he once fucked his Mary in it. I smile smugly as I back away admiring my parting legacy, but as soon as I click the cottage door closed behind me, my breath quivers. All I need to do is hold it together until I make it clear of the common. I came here to lift my Christmas spirit, to prepare myself for spending tomorrow alone, but I'm no better off than when I arrived, in fact, I think I'm worse.

Chapter Eighteen

Gabriel

I rub my hands together vigorously to spark the blood flow. Saying goodbye to Olivia took longer than expected, but it was the closure I needed. Most importantly, it helped me rationalise my feelings for Penny and how important what she did or didn't tell me about Henry really is. She didn't leave with him, she stayed, she saw the nativity through, and she wants to talk. And for all of those reasons and more, I know I made the right decision opening my heart to her.

I slow as I make my way along the aisle towards the stage, and I glance quickly at my phone. *Shit.* It's so much later than I realised.

'Ah, Gabriel. Merry Christmas,' Helen says, waddling towards me with a massive bunch of flowers that my father buys her every year. 'I'll see you next year?'

'Of course,' I say, scratching my head. 'Err, Helen? Have you seen Penny?'

She thrusts her bouquet in the direction I've just come from and my stomach twists in knots. 'She was outside with your brother and the twins waving off the donkey, but after that I don't know. Anyway, I really must get home, I need to get the turkey in.'

I force an agreeable smile, but anyone that cooks their turkey the day before and reheats it clearly lives on the edge. 'Thanks, Helen.'

I pull my phone from my back pocket and sink into one of the hard church seats; how anyone enjoys a nativity in these uncomfortable chairs I'll never know. I toss my head back, stifling a regretful laugh. 'I don't even have her shitting number,' I say out loud.

I'm doused in a pool of light as the door to my father's office opens up and my whole family emerge.

'Gabriel. It was so wonderful, a transformation. We must have Penny back next year, I don't think we can top it, she was a vision,' my father cries.

'Well, that will be up to Penny, won't it? Unfortunately I've no clue where she is, but by all means ask her.'

'What do you mean? She was outside with us, but she disappeared, figured she went to talk to you, maybe she thought you and Olivia needed a moment,' Adam mumbles as he busies himself zipping up the girls' coats.

I shoot upright in the chair as my heart pounds in my chest. 'She saw me with Olivia?'

'Olivia?' my mother repeats in surprise.

'Fuck.' I jump to my feet and race to the doors, charging through them without daring to stop.

'Penny!' I shout, my voice echoing across the common. I turn in search of the petrol can, but it's gone and my heart sinks. 'No...' I double over and shake my head in disbelief. How is this happening?

'Come on, she might be back at the cottage if you hurry.' Adam's hand connects with my shoulder in a tight squeeze.

I drag my eyes up to his and he nods encouragingly. 'Come on, if she's there and you miss her by being dramatic, you'll kick yourself.'

❄

'Pen...Pen?' I call her name as I charge through the cottage door. 'Billy?'

The stairs rumble as I take them two at a time. When I hit the bedroom, I know I'm too late.

'Gabriel!' Adam calls.

I drag myself back downstairs and he stands with the veil in his hands. 'She's been here, you know. She left this.'

'I know, all her stuff's gone.'

'Call her!'

'I don't have her number.'

'You're telling me you've been sleeping with this woman, and you don't have her phone number?'

Anger simmers in my chest. 'It wasn't exactly a conventional meeting, was it? I didn't date her, she didn't come back here and fall into bed after a late night of dancing and drinks. She was a stranger – we were sharing a bed, reluctantly, because we had no choice.'

'Until?'

'Until things changed.'

He smiles in understanding. 'You shared a bed the whole time?'

'Pretty much.' I sink deflated to the couch.

'Camping bed break, did it?'

'Yeah, how do you know?' I draw my brows in question.

'I loosened the screws.'

I turn slowly to stare at him. 'When?'

'2009'

'2009?' I repeat slowly.

'Yeah, you were going on that fishing trip with Dad and I wasn't allowed to go, and I got the raving hump about it, so I loosened the screws.'

My eyes widen as I take in the absolute ridiculousness of his story. 'We never went.'

'I know.' He laughs. 'I completely forgot about it until Mum told me about Penny turning up. I can't tell you how excited I was going to bed that night, imagining you ending up flat on your arse.'

I point at him and sink my teeth into my bottom lip. 'Those girls are going to turn out just like you, I know it.'

'I hope they do.' He grins.

'You absolute fucker.'

'A thanks would be nice.'

I shake my head. 'It's too late. I've lost her by not speaking up and saying anything, as per usual.'

Adam runs the fabric of the veil over in his hand and bites down hard on his lower lip.

'Where did she leave that?' I ask, pointing towards her parting gift.

'Here on the rocking chair.'

I smile to myself. Whatever she was thinking when she left, one's things for certain, it wasn't regret.

'What's that look about?'

'Nothing,' I say innocently, my eye scanning the length of the rocking chair and back up again.

'Oh god,' Adam cries, jumping from the seat. 'You absolute animals, I don't even want to know how the logistics of that work.'

'Hey, don't rock it til you try it.' I raise my brows triumphantly.

'How did you even convince her?' He scratches his head as he pushes the frame with his foot. 'If she was up for that she's a keeper.'

'She is...was.'

'You need to go after her...like now,' he says, tossing the veil at me.

I stand abruptly, throwing it to one side. 'I don't know where she lives, do I?'

'Oh shit. Yeah.'

I yank open the fridge and knock Billy's food bowl with the door, scattering dry food everywhere. *She was in such a rush, she didn't even take the poor sod's food.*

'Wait!' Adam cries.

I pause, lowering the beer which was inches away from my lips.

'What?' I sigh.

'Mum, she'll have her address from the booking.'

'No, Henry booked it.'

'Yeah, and they were engaged, right, they obviously lived together?'

Shit, he's right. I discard the beer bottle on the side and grab my coat, patting it down for my car keys.

'You're going after her?'

'I've got to try, haven't I?'

The December chill stings my face as I storm along the path and unlock my car.

'You need the address,' Adam shouts as I slam the car door shut.

I turn over the ignition and lower the window. 'Text it to me. I can't afford to wait.'

The wheels spin and screech against the icy terrain and

nerves hit as I wonder how she even made it out of the common in these conditions. She can't have got far, but it doesn't matter if she has, I'd travel anywhere. Because this time I'm not going to let distance destroy my chance of happiness.

Chapter Nineteen

Penny

'Driving Home for Christmas' blasts from the car radio and the only reason I haven't switched stations is because it's drowning out my pathetic sniffling. I can most definitely wait to see their faces because I wasn't expecting to see them. In my head my Christmas was playing out one very specific way and this wasn't it. Stuck in motorway traffic on Christmas Eve after the most unexpected yet incredible few days I've ever had. The memory of Mistletoe Cottage will lessen over time, but Gabriel Harris will be imprinted on my brain for a lifetime. I didn't ask for a holiday romance, but I was delivered one, nevertheless. Images of Molly with Henry flash vividly in my mind and I'm merely left with regret at all the years wasted, but my stomach then rolls as Gabriel and Olivia thrust to the forefront of my consciousness. Some people are meant to have second chances and clearly, they're those people. Maybe I'm just someone who's destined to have lots of happiness, but not ever afters.

I shift uncomfortably in my seat as my legs start to go numb from lack of movement. At this rate it will be next Christmas by the time I get to my parents'. I hit the voice command and announce loudly that I want to call Mum and Dad and wait for it to connect.

'Penny!' my mum screeches loudly as the phone connects, waking Billy from his slumber.

'Yeah, hi, Mum.'

'What on earth are you doing? Henry came to rescue you and said you were shacked up with some man, playing the Virgin Mary. He said he threatened him with violence.'

I scrunch my face up, that doesn't sound right.

'No...that's not...wait, is Henry there?'

'Yes, of course, he's worried about you.'

'Worried? He wasn't that worried when he was having sex with Molly behind my back, and then changing the locks on our home five days ago, leaving me stranded, was he?'

The line goes silent, and I jolt in surprise as cars around me start to sound their horns. *Crap.* I force the car into gear and inch forward in the slow-moving traffic.

'Mum...Mum...what's going on?'

'It's your dad, he's escorting him out.'

I wince as I imagine the scene. My dad's not a force to be reckoned with. If Henry wants to be concerned about anyone's wrath, it's his.

I strain to hear the faint chatter over the noise of the traffic as the road finally opens up ahead of me.

'Mum?' I ask once more.

'Hello, love, it's me.'

'Dad...' Tears well in my eyes as I hear the voice of the one man I know will never hurt me or let me down.

'Pen, I'm not going to pretend I'm happy about you staying with a stranger in the middle of nowhere, but that's down to Henry, he's a lot to answer for. I've got the keys to your flat. He said Molly's gone and I told him if he dares turn up on your doorstep again that he'll have me to deal with, so if you want to go home you can.'

'Thank you,' I force out, wiping the tears clear from my cheeks.

'You hang up now. We'll see you soon, back home where you belong.'

The radio cuts back in as the calls ends and 'Away in a Manger' starts to play through the speakers. I drop my eyes briefly to my costume and laugh softly to myself. If only Gabriel could see me now.

Gabriel

'Twenty-four, Joseph Street, St Mary's Bay—'

'Are you taking the piss?' I cry out as I steam down the motorway.

'No, straight up, this is the address Mum gave me.'

I shake my head in disbelief. You'd have thought this would have been something she mentioned, as a quirky little coincidence, but no, she's been a complete closed book the whole time. Dedicated to the nativity and that alone.

'Fine, look just text me the post code, I'll pick it up from that.'

'Good luck, mate.'

'I'm going to need it. I offered to rearrange the bloke's face a few hours ago, he might not even tell me where she is.'

'As I said, good luck.' Adam laughs.

A few moments after the call ends the message comes through and I instruct the sat nav to reroute to that address. *St Mary's Bay.* Unbelievable...but then nothing about the last few days has been normal. A stream of taillights brake ahead of me and I groan, tipping my head back against the headrest. This is why I travel to Christmas Common early every single year, I can't abide holiday traffic, but this is different, I'd sit in this all night for even the slimmest of chances that she'll hear me out.

❄

Nearly three hours later, I pull up on Joseph Street. Cars line either side of the road and under the dim streetlighting I can barely make out the numbers that adorn the brick walls. Still, it's lighter than the common. A Christmas tree illuminates the front window of every home I pass, and I come to a steady stop as I spot one in darkness. 24.

I pause at the end of the path and glance up at the darkened windows. If I've travelled all this way and that bastard isn't even home, I swear to god...

I march towards the front door, gathering momentum, staring straight ahead. My ankle twists and I find myself careering forward, landing with a thud against the door. I look back in a daze at the offending item I had the misfortune of clipping my foot on and my breath catches – I've never been more relieved to see a cat carrier in all my life.

'Gabriel?' Penny sniffs as she looms over me.

Scrambling to my feet, I dust myself off. My anxious heart starts to settle, and I hoist the empty cat carrier and peer inside. 'Oh, thank Christ, I thought I'd killed him.'

She laughs softly, whilst clinging firmly to the door. 'I mean how many lives do you want to try and rob him of in a week?'

I smile weakly and thrust the carrier towards her.

'He's inside asleep, I just left it out here.'

I nod. 'Is there anyone else here or...?'

'If you mean Henry, no, my dad sorted him out.'

My conflicted heart hammers at the knowledge that she's alone. Pleased that she didn't go back to him, and saddened that if I'd never tracked her down, she'd have chosen to spend the holiday by herself.

'I'm sorry, what are you doing here and how did you find me?' she asks, wrapping her dressing gown tightly around her body, in the same way I've watched her do time and time again over the last few days.

'Mum got the address from the booking?'

'Isn't that some kind of data protection breach?'

Of all the things she could be worried about right now. 'I'm not selling your information on, it's for personal use.' I roll my eyes.

'Personal how?' Her eyes narrow.

'Look, can I come in? I need to talk to you.'

'Olivia not with you?' she forces out.

An air of jealousy hovers between us and I can't help but laugh even though there's nothing remotely funny about it. 'There is no Olivia.'

'But I saw you both—'

'Yet here I am...with you.'

Her throat bobs as she swallows hard, and there's nothing I want to do more than take her in my arms and kiss her fears away, but I'll be damned if I'm laying another finger on her until I know that her heart is mine.

'Please let me in, Pen.'

Her eyes glisten as her name passes my lips and with one sweeping movement, she steps back, inviting me in.

'I need to let you know though, if you're thinking of staying, I'm getting the airbed out.'

Chapter Twenty

Penny

We sit opposite one another, our hands clasped around steaming mugs of tea. I glance casually at my phone and as the minutes count down to midnight the silence becomes heavier.

'I—' we both say.

'Sorry, you first,' Gabriel rushes out.

'No, it's fine, you came to see me so...'

He leans forward in his chair, settling his mug on the floor. 'We never got to talk after the nativity... You were great by the way, everyone wants you back.'

'Everyone?'

'Yes. W-we all d-do. Especially me.' He rubs his thighs as his voice quivers.

I shake my head as I imagine making the trip to Christmas Common the same way he does every year. After the time we've spent together, how exactly am I supposed to forget that he exists for 364 days a year and suppress my feelings for the other one.

'I don't think it's going to work.'

His face falls as panic sets in. 'I'm willing to try – you're worth it. I wouldn't be here otherwise. We've both been hurt, and I know things are more raw for you than they are for me with tomorrow having been your wedding day and all, but I don't know about you but the last few days, I've never been happier.'

My rapid pulse thunders around my body as I try and decipher what he's really getting at, because the last thing I want, or need, is to be made a fool of...again.

'Are you talking about the nativity?'

'What? No...I'm talking about us, you and me. I thought you...I hoped you might feel the same?'

I fight hard against my smile that's desperate to break out. 'And how do you feel?'

Standing abruptly, he sighs heavily, his stare pinning me with the same intensity that it has numerous times over the last few days.

'That I don't want to be alone at Christmas anymore, or at all for that matter. And I don't know the logistics of this' – he flicks his finger back and forth between us and takes my chin between his thumb and his forefinger – 'but I'm willing to take a chance, in the hope that this time next Christmas, I wake up with you in my arms.'

I stand and his large warm hands slide up into my hair as our foreheads connect.

'I want that too,' I whisper against his lips.

His mouth gently takes mine in a kiss that's tender, unhurried and full of promise. I mould my body into his and he drops his hands, allowing them to snake around my waist, pinning me close.

'I never want to let you go, Pen.'

'Then don't.' I smile.

He laughs softly and the vibrations travel along my jaw and down my spine. He starts to walk us backwards, blindly navigating a flat he doesn't know.

'Are...you...looking...for...the...airbed?' I ask between kisses.

'Am I fuck. Show me your bed right now.'

Gabriel

I drop Penny to the mattress, and she bounces lightly against the springs. Falling to my knees, I turn my head to the side where I find her discarded costume lying in a pile in the corner. I tug swiftly at the cord to her dressing gown, and it falls open, leaving her in nothing but her underwear. I lower my lips to her bare thigh and kiss her.

'You know, that's church property,' I say, nipping at her skin.

A small gasp escapes her lips as she falls back against the sheets. 'What are you going to do about it?'

'I don't know...help you repent your sins.' I slide my body up over hers and as soon as my cock grazes over the lace of her underwear, my resolve slips. 'I was going to drag this out, but I-I can't wait any longer for you.'

'Good, take me, I'm yours,' she forces out between heavy breaths.

I hook my fingers into the elastic of the lace and slip them down her legs. I stand, discarding all my clothing, mesmerised as she rolls on to her front and wiggles her behind at me. I take a condom from my wallet and as I take my dick in my hand, I don't think I've ever been harder than I am right now. I pin my eyes closed as I slowly roll it down my length, because if I keep looking at the perfect curve of her body laid out before me, I don't think this will be the reunion she was hoping for.

She turns coyly and raises her hips towards me.

'From behind, like the first time,' she asks, wiggling her eyebrows.

Fuck yes. Without hesitation, I cover her body with mine and sink deep inside her with one powerful thrust. I reach up, taking her hand in mine, locking our fingers as I inch my cock slowly out and back in, over and over until her insides clench tightly around me.

'Gabriel,' her muffled voice cries into the mattress.

'I know,' I murmur.

Her hands claw at the sheets and her desperation for release spurs me on. Thrust after thrust, I give her everything I've got, because now she has all of me. We belong to each other.

I still as her body detonates around mine and I slow my pace until she's completely reacclimatised to her surroundings, then finally, I let myself go.

❄

There's a soft thud at the foot of the bed and we both crane our necks to greet our bedtime companion.

'Are you okay if he sleeps in here. You really have nothing to be afraid of,' Penny says, running her fingers mindlessly across my chest.

'I know. We actually had a moment before the nativity, I allowed him within a foot of me and he didn't kill me. He did headbutt me though.'

Penny's body tenses and her fingertips dig into my skin. 'Oh, that means he loves you.'

'How do you know that?' I ask, rolling my eyes. 'Cat whisperer, are you?'

'No. I just know.'

She pushes herself up onto her elbow and looks down at me and for a second, I think she's going to say something but then she drops her head to mine, nudging it slightly before slipping back into the crook of my arm.

My heart thunders in my chest and I could very well say it out loud, but sometimes you know it isn't necessary. I drop my lips to her forehead and place a gentle kiss before nudging her back. We both laugh softly and hold on to each other a little bit tighter.

Epilogue

Penny

Twelve whole months of trips up and down the motorway. Weekends that are too short and holidays that are few and far between, but in exactly five minutes, I'll be back at Mistletoe Cottage.

'Are you looking forward to seeing Gabriel, Billy?'

Meep.

Of course. Because the man who fears cats, is no more. He's been cured, one headbutt at a time. So much so that they gang up on me on any given opportunity. In the height of summer, we spent a week in Greece and Gabriel even booked Billy into a cat hotel that FaceTimes you so you can talk to them. They're officially each other's partner in crime.

By the time I've pulled up outside the cottage my cheeks are aching from being unable to contain my grin. I could spot Gabriel a mile off, hovering outside, waiting for us.

'What are you doing? Go inside it's freezing,' I say as I lower the window.

'I'm sorry, who are you, do you have a booking?' He smirks.

'Ha. Very funny. Make yourself useful and open the boot, it's full of presents.'

I stare at him in the mirrors from every angle as he approaches the rear of the car. They say the honeymoon phase is short lived, but I can confirm it isn't, and I didn't even need to get married in the first place to experience it. Everything worked out just the way it was supposed to.

I grind to a halt as I enter the cottage; it's like entering a different home.

'Like it?' Gabriel asks, sidling up behind me.

The twinkle of lights and the scent of a new tree lingers in the air, whilst a pot of mulled wine simmers away on the stove.

'Like it?' I turn in his arms. 'I love it.'

'And I love you, Penny Hastings.'

He backs me into the lounge area and the warmth from the fireplace licks at my skin. 'What are you doing? I need to unpack.' I giggle.

'I need you seated...' he says, positioning me in front of the rocking chair.

'Oh yeah?' I wink.

'Penny...control yourself.'

A wicked smile creeps across his face and he disappears upstairs. I grip the arms of the chair tightly and with each gentle rock I shift, trying to get comfortable, whilst imagining all of the ways that tonight is going to be different to this time last year. Holding down something long distance is hard, but it definitely makes the reunions sweeter.

'Close your eyes,' Gabriel calls out.

My pulse doubles in anticipation and I dutifully oblige. Things are about to get exciting.

'Billy, come here,' I hear Gabriel whisper.

I scrunch my face in confusion. They may be best buds now,

but Gabriel always draws a line at having Billy in the room whilst we're having sex.

A rustling at my feet has me retracting, curling up into the chair. 'Gabriel...I don't like this.'

'Shhh, it's okay.' His hand connects with mine and he pulls me towards him. 'Here, open your eyes.'

They widen instantly and there in Gabriel's strong muscular arms is the teeniest, tiniest kitten I've ever laid my eyes on. Billy wasn't even this small when we got him.

'I know Christmas is a few days away, but I couldn't hide him for that long.'

I bounce, eagerly reaching out as Gabriel places him in my arms. 'Is he ours?'

'Of course.'

Billy jumps to my lap and sniffs curiously. I hold my breath and wait, this is make or break, if Billy doesn't like him then...

'Ah, that's my boy.' Gabriel ruffles Billy's head as he gently nudges the kitten and gives him a welcoming lick. 'What a greeting.'

Gabriel drags two new cat beds from underneath the tree and settles them in front of the fireplace. 'Here you go. They'll love it, basking together.'

I launch myself from the chair and gently place our new arrival in the comfort of his padded bed and as soon as I release him, Billy's all over him. 'It's perfect. You're perfect,' I whisper.

Gabriel throws his arm around me and pulls me close, nuzzling his face into my hair. The thud of his heart hammers underneath my fingertips and I know this sensation all too well. He's biding his time, but any second now he's going to start something that won't be finished for hours. His mouth drops to mine in a searing kiss, and I squeal as he bends and lifts me until my legs are wrapped tightly around his waist. I glance over his shoulder as he carries me towards the stairs. This time last year I was going to bed alone, but looking back I couldn't be more grateful for a broken camping bed and an inquisitive cat. Because neither of us are spending Christmas alone.

❄

The sheets cling to my body as I throw my head back against the pillow. We've been up here for hours and downstairs is suspiciously quiet, and with a new kitten, there's sure to be trouble.

'Shall I check on them?'

'Leave them, they'll be sleeping,' Gabriel murmurs as he runs his fingers through my hair.

'Like we should. We have rehearsals tomorrow.'

'We don't need rehearsals. It's you and me.'

Last year's nativity turned out to be so popular that this year Charles is having to put on a matinee as well. People are flocking from far and wide to watch the first real-life couple play Mary and Joseph in nearly a decade. 'But we're twice as busy this year and—'

'All the more reason for us to spend this quality time together.' His hand travels down my body and my senses reawaken. As he presses himself to my side, how hard he has become already is glaringly obvious.

I reach out and my face falls as I shake the empty condom box and hold it out between us. 'What now?' I shrug.

'I think we should ditch them – we've been together a year almost – what do you say?'

I lean back to take in his whole face, and butterflies swirl in my stomach in preparation for this conversation.

'But if something happens, we're not living together.'

'Well perhaps we should live together then?'

'But I'd like to be married first.'

His eyebrows raise and he smiles softly. 'Noted.'

'Gabriel...' I cry, swatting him playfully.

'Shall we take a leap together, you, me and the cats?' he asks.

My breath catches as I reach out, running my hand across his face. 'Have we known each other long enough?'

'I think back to this time last year, Penny, and every moment we've shared in between, and there's no one I'd rather be doing life with than you, nativities included. So, what do you say, Pen, can you spend every day with me as well as every Christmas?'

I roll my lips, desperately trying to contain the eagerness of my smile, because waking up with Gabriel and my boys each morning would be like having my own little slice of heaven.

'Is that a yes, Penny Hastings?' he says, pulling me in close.

I hold his face between my hands and take his lips in a slow, promising kiss.

'It's a yes... I mean, it's not like you're a stranger, is it?'

The End

Afterword

Thank you so much for reading Away with a Stranger. If you enjoyed reading about what Penny, Gabriel and Billy got up to, then please consider leaving a review. Reviews mean everything to authors!

Acknowledgments

I should really start by thanking my fiancé, who once again has been my biggest supporter. To have someone who not only takes an interest but cheers you on even when things don't go the way you planned, means the world. You're my rock.

I'd like to say a huge thank you to my beta team, Britt, Chels and Tash, thank you for your feedback and for reading a Christmas novella in the middle of summer (sorry not sorry Tash.) You tell me when things work and when they don't, and most importantly, you tell me when to take a break, so thank you for being there at every step.

A special thank you to Lee at Coffin Print Designs for managing to capture Penny, Gabriel and Billy in the best way possible. When you send a message saying you want a Christmas cover, with nativity vibes and a cat...you think you're asking the impossible, but you pulled it off!

Once again a massive thank you to my editor, Aimee. For helping make this book what it is and for steering me in the right direction when things go wrong. I'd be lost without you.

To Ellie and Melissa, our group chat feels like our own little cheering squad. It's been a privilege getting to work with you both this year!

Finally, but by no means least, Billy. You're the most precious boy and give the worlds best headbutts.

Louise x

About the Author

Louise Hudson adores all things romance, from musicals, to films and most importantly books. Her kindle is permanently by her side so she can steal every spare opportunity to catch up on reading. Having discovered her love of storytelling at a young age, she decided it was now time to start sharing her characters with the world.

Also by Louise Hudson

Always Beth

She missed out on her happily ever after.

He's not sure if he deserves one.

Sometimes, fate needs a helping hand…

Printed in Great Britain
by Amazon

31656431R10081